The Schoolmaster's Bride

The Schoolmaster's Bride

MEREDITH RESCE

Golden Grain Publishing

The Schoolmaster's Bride
Copyright © 2006 Meredith Resce

Golden Grain Publishing

PO Box 106, Reynella SA 5161

The National Library of Australia Cataloguing-in-Publication Information:

Resce, Meredith, 1963 -.
The schoolmaster's bride.

ISBN 9780977592708.

ISBN 0 9775927 0 7.

I. Title.

A823.3

This is a work of fiction. Names, characters and incidents are either the product of the author's imagination or are used fictiously, and any resemblance to actual events or persons, living or dead, is entirely coincidental.

Printed In South Australia by HYDE PARK PRESS
First Printing October 2006

Christian Fiction; Period Drama; Romance.

Cover Design: Matthew Holmes
Photograph: Dave Scarallo
Back cover Photograph used with kind permission of the Melrose Districts History Society Inc

Acknowledgements

Thanks as always to the family, especially Elisa, whose talents as a critic are excellent. Thanks, Pat Mayfield for your editing expertise, Matthew Holmes for your design ideas, Dave Scarallo for photos on demand, Mike and Colleen Morgan for location on demand, Ed Darwood for always being available to proof-read, and Ken Linn and the team at Hyde Park Press for your professional attitude.

About The Author

South Australian author, Meredith Resce, has been writing for sixteen years, and has had books in the Australian market since 1997.

Following the Australian success of her "Heart of Green Valley" series, English Publisher, Authentic Media, have contracted the first three books in the series, and have released them to the British and American markets.

Apart from writing, Meredith also takes the opportunity to speak to groups on issues relevant to relationships and emotional and spiritual growth.

With her husband, Nick, she works with Edge Church International, co-ordinating different creative projects, running the drama team and preaching occasionally.

Meredith and Nick have one daughter and two sons

Chapter One

Rural South Australia - 1933

D ianne suddenly came to her senses as the sound of the puffing steam engine faded into the night. She had been watching the two or three other people who had left the train get into the various vehicles that had been there waiting for them. Now everybody had gone, and she suddenly realised that she was left standing alone on the platform. She pulled her woollen coat closer around her ears as the chill of the night began to penetrate, and she shivered involuntarily. The sun had completely disappeared behind the hills to the west, and the light was fast fading into a dull twilight.

"S'cuse me, lady."

Dianne turned around quickly as a man spoke behind her.

"Sorry to startle you, ma'm," he apologised. "Was just wondering if you were expecting to meet someone."

Dianne had been dumbfounded by the question. Of course she had been expecting someone to meet her, and as the station master spoke it became apparent that no-one was there for her. For just a few moments her confidence was shaken, and it took her a couple of deep steadying breaths for her to regain her composure.

"I'm sorry!" Dianne began. "My name is Mrs. Pierceson. I'm the new school teacher for the Carlton Public School."

The stationmaster nodded in acknowledgement, touching his hat as a courtesy.

Dianne waited, expecting an explanation or directive, but he didn't appear to have anything to add. He shifted about self consciously before turning back toward the small hut that graced the top of the short platform.

"Sir, excuse me," Dianne called after him, "Is there someone going to meet me?"

He stopped and turned back to face her, still looking uncomfortable.

"It doesn't seem like it, Mrs Pierceson, I'm sorry."

At first Dianne was annoyed, and then a little panicky, but once again, a couple of deep breaths and she was able to take control of her rising emotions. "Would you be so kind as to direct me to the school then, please."

Even as she spoke she realised that, apart from the small station house and the sign bearing the word *Carlton*, there was no other building or sign of a town in the immediate vicinity. The panic resurfaced and it must have shown on her face as the little man offered an explanation.

"The township is about a mile and a half up the road, Mrs. Pierceson. If you follow this track up that direction about a hundred yards, you'll come to the main road. Turn left and keep going. You'll come to the town sooner or later."

Sooner or later, Dianne thought to herself, not exactly reassured by the directions, but she swallowed her indignation in an effort to remain civil.

"I beg your pardon sir," she continued, "but isn't there any transport that could take me to the town? I doubt I could carry my luggage from here to that hut, let alone a mile and a half."

"Sorry, Mrs Pierceson." He apologised again.

"I can pay you," she hurried on, the fear beginning to overtake her adopted confidence.

"Won't do any good," he commented dryly. "I live here in that 'little hut', as you call it, and don't have any transport apart from my own two legs, which seem to serve me well enough."

He turned back to his hut, and began to stack her luggage, that had been tossed onto the platform from the passenger train, into a tidy pile under the small verandah. "When you get to town," he mumbled, "you can send someone out to pick up your things. I'll keep my eye on them until then."

Dianne was rendered speechless by his indifference, and simply stared at him as he dragged her large, leather-bound trunk up next to the wall. By the time she'd fully realised what was happening, she'd become quite angry, but thankfully, commonsense prevailed, and she was prevented from unleashing her frustration upon the little stationmaster who, she reasoned, was not only unable to help her nor was he responsible for her predicament. She turned from him, unhappy about the way things had turned out so far, but sensible enough not to blame her troubles on the wrong person.

As she began to trudge down the station track, she began to ask herself just who was responsible for this predicament. She knew that she'd written informing the schoolmaster of her date of arrival, and had understood from the letter she'd received that he was expecting her. But as to who was actually responsible for leaving her unwelcomed and without introduction or transport to her new home, she didn't quite know where to aim her displeasure.

It had been over twenty-four hours since the passenger train had pulled out of the distant city railway station. Other passengers had leaned from the open carriage windows, some calling goodbye, others weeping as they waved their handkerchiefs, all seeming to promise a hasty return. But Dianne had sat back in her seat. She had arrived at the station in company with her father-in-law, and though he had wished her well, he hadn't waited with her. She knew that part of her life was over and that she would not be returning. She had hopes of a new start, and it was that hope that kept her looking forward with anticipation, rather than backward with regret.

The dull twilight had faded into pitch dark by the time Dianne reached the outskirts of the town. She had managed to use almost every last ounce of her will power not to scream aloud in panic. She was alone, walking in the dark in a strange place. She didn't really know where she was going, or what she would find there, or even if she would ever find the place. As she eventually reached the town limits, she suddenly realised why she had not been able to see it as she approached from a distance. There were no street lights. The light glowing from the windows of the small houses was not the bright cheery aura of electric light, but obviously the dim flickering light of a kerosene lamp.

Quite suddenly Dianne could sense the irony of her situation. She and Samuel had always appreciated the modern conveniences of life, and had secretly scoffed at the older generation who had resisted the changes that scientific advancement had brought. And now, here she was, in the very centre of backward thinking. But then she realised that perhaps she wasn't being fair. Perhaps electricity hadn't made it out to this part of the country yet. Perhaps other people in the town were better set up, and had the benefit of modern equipment. She kept walking, knowing that in a short time she would find out.

A dog barked at her as she passed by a small cottage with a picket fence. Though she could just see the outline of the house there was nothing in particular to distinguish it from other houses. A dim light glowed in the small window beneath an overhanging verandah, and the pungent smell of chimney smoke wafted down to remind her that she was standing outdoors on a cold autumn evening, while a blazing fire most likely burned in the grate of this and all the other houses in this unfamiliar town.

Dianne still had no idea how far she was from the schoolhouse, nor if anyone would even be there when she arrived. In her mind she knew she had no better option than to make enquiries, and this house was as good a place as any to start. She fumbled with the latch on the picket fence gate, opened it, and began to walk up the short garden path, talking to herself in an attempt to conquer her dismay and give an appearance of confidence. She banished stray thoughts that she might find somebody unfriendly, or worse still, aggressive or even dangerous. These were the sorts of thoughts that would constantly emerge from her active imagination, and it took considerable willpower to squash them before they put her in a real fright. But squash them she did, and by the time she'd knocked at the front door, she had convinced herself that she would find a friendly, helpful person. Of course the small dog that had first barked at her was hard to ignore in all of her imaginings, as he rushed up and down the side fence that separated them, in an absolute frenzy of barking.

"Ssh! Be quiet, pup!" She spoke in her best teacher's voice. But no matter how stern she had thought her tone to be, the little dog continued to yap and growl, and didn't stop until a gruff voice from inside called to it.

"Be quiet dog – you blasted mongrel!"

Dianne was shocked at the coarse language, but recovered her wits by the time the hefty, middle-aged man had fully opened the door.

"Who's there?" His deep resounding voice seemed to boom at her.

"I'm sorry to have disturbed you at this time of night," Dianne began, trying to sound polite, and not completely terrified. "I have just arrived from the city, and am expected by the Schoolmaster ... "

She was cut off rudely by a loud guffaw, as the man threw back his head as if she'd made a good joke.

"The schoolmaster you say," he blurted in his amusement. "Now what sort of woman would you be to be coming to him in the dark of night, might I ask?"

"I resent your remarks sir," she retorted hotly. "I am a decent, upstanding, Christian woman, and have been engaged here in Carlton as the new teacher." She paused to allow this to impress him. "And I'm certain that your schoolmaster is also a man of good character."

"I beg your pardon, Miss." The huge man seemed instantly subdued, as if he'd suddenly realised he'd made a great blunder. "I'm sure you're quite respectable, but as to the schoolmaster, obviously you've never met him or you'd know he's a man of questionable principles and virtues."

Dianne heard what he said, and couldn't fail to understand what he meant, but she tried to dismiss the words as misguided. She had already realised this man could speak out of turn and be way off the truth, so she decided to ignore his comments about the schoolmaster.

"I'm sorry to trouble you, sir," she went on as calmly as her ruffled emotions would allow. "If you could direct me to the schoolmaster's residence, then I will be on my way."

"Only too glad to help Miss..."

"Mrs. Pierceson," she corrected him. "And you are...?" she paused expectantly for a reply.

"Folks call me Tom," he answered quickly. "Now if you keep on the same path, you've only another five or six houses to pass before you'll see the Carlton Public School. It's the same side of the road as my place. The schoolmaster's house is attached to the side, so you won't miss it, Mrs. Pierceson."

"Thank you!" Dianne tried to sound grateful even though she was struggling with the resentment still burning from the earlier insult.

"Hope you won't hold my hasty words against me, Missus." Tom lowered his tone to a worried whisper. "My good wife often scolds me for my impertinence."

Dianne nodded in acknowledgment of the attempted apology.

"And I hope you can get on with that there man, for I'm sure no-one else can work him out."

Dianne hurried away from Tom's cottage back into the street, carefully reciting to herself the directions she'd just been given, and trying to forget what he'd said about her new employer.

As she moved on down the dusty road, which was obviously the main street, she acknowledged an eerie feeling about the small town, with its people snug in the safety of their own homes, away from the intense black of the night. And she, a stranger, was left to squint her eyes in an effort to make out the buildings as she passed them, hoping she would be able to recognise the schoolhouse when she came upon it.

I'm sure the school board is not going to retain a master whose morals and methods are not completely above reproach, Dianne thought to herself, desperately trying to reason away the doubts and fears that her imagination had begun to elaborate upon. *Of course not,* she chided her own fertile imagination. *Of course that was just ridiculous gossip.*

She was thankful that she had reached what could only be the schoolhouse, for it distracted her from her disconcerting thoughts. Just as Tom had told her, there was a residence attached to the side. The night was so dark that Dianne could only just see the outline of the building in the dim starlight. She guessed that it was a stone building, judging by its looming size. But what the building looked like was hardly her first thought as she was more worried about the fact that she would have to arrive unannounced on a stranger's doorstep. She wondered again how it was that he had not anticipated her arrival, and why he had not sent someone to meet her at the station.

Summoning every bit of courage she possessed, Dianne approached the front door of the schoolmaster's residence, reached up and sounded the knocker against the door.

"Who's that?" A deep resounding voice, not unlike Tom's, thundered from behind the closed door.

At first, Dianne resented the way everybody seemed to call out aggressively from behind closed doors, and was reluctant to answer. But then her reason reminded her that they couldn't possibly know who was knocking at their door at night.

"It's Mrs. Pierceson. I've just arrived from the city," she replied, trying to sound confident and in charge, when in fact she was wishing that the ground would open and swallow her. "There was no-one at the station to meet me…"

Before she could finish her explanation the front door opened and a shaft of lamp light nearly blinded her after having been in the dark for so long. It took her eyes a few moments to recover and adjust, and then she was able to see a tall imposing figure standing in the doorway. The lamp he held in his hand cast strange shadows on the man's face, and coupled with the fact that he wore a severe frown was enough to set Dianne's imagination running wild. The memory of Tom's recent assessment only added to this new state of fright.

"I didn't know there'd be a wife along," the man blurted inhospitably. "You'll have to make arrangements for your own accommodation tomorrow, as I'm sure Mrs. Todd was not expecting a married couple. You can stay with her tonight, I daresay, right across the street, and tell Mr. Pierceson I'll expect him in my class room at eight am sharp."

With no more than a cursory nod he simply closed the door in her face leaving Dianne's fear replaced by utter astonishment.

"What a rude man!" she finally observed out loud. There had been no greeting, no apology or explanation. She could hardly believe that she had been summarily dismissed without so much as a 'how do you do'. For a few moments she considered knocking on the door again and demanding a proper reception. But then she didn't think she had the emotional energy to go through that exercise again, and she still had to find Mrs Todd's house and make explanations.

Sighing with the indignity of it all, she turned on her heel and headed back down the short path to the dusty street. Straining her eyes in the darkness she eventually saw there was only one building in the general vicinity that occupied the opposite side of the street, and she supposed it had to be Mrs. Todd's residence. But that was all she knew: she had no inkling who Mrs Todd could be, or what position she might hold.

Chapter Two

It had been a very strange night. Once Mrs Mary-Ann Todd had opened the door to her and understood what had happened, she had gone into a flurry, mixing her apologies with busy activity, preparing food, making another pot of tea, and generally expressing her dissatisfaction with the way the whole affair had been handled. It was very obvious to Dianne that Mrs Todd did not approve of the schoolmaster at all. She had described him using many derogatory terms while her husband, Peter Todd, gently and methodically contradicted her after each outburst. Dianne had been shown a bed in the Todds' prepared spare room, her head whirling with information. The Todds had been expecting to board the new teacher, and although they had expected a man, they had not been told exactly which day he was to arrive. Dianne said nothing about not being a man, and hoped that it meant nothing. She also offered her apology, saying that she had sent the instructions about when she would arrive, and now assumed that the letter must have gone astray. Mary-Ann had her doubts and was not quite so generous in letting the schoolmaster off the hook.

Dianne liked both Mr and Mrs Todd immediately. They were kind, generous people, unless of course in the case of the schoolmaster, and it was Mary-Ann speaking. The Todds were in their mid-sixties, and told Dianne that they had

retired from the land and come to live in the town. Peter
Todd was a cheerful, positive sort of person. He didn't have a
lot to say, but when he did, it was always sensible. Mary-Ann,
on the other hand, had an opinion about everything. Oh, she
was a generous sort of woman, but was loud and direct on
any subject, and displayed various emotions, each of which
reflected the rapid changes in her topic of conversation.

When Mary-Ann placed an enormous breakfast in front
of her, Dianne had balked. She had never been a large eater,
and in the previous years of scarcity, she had eaten even less.
But Mary-Ann's assessment of the situation was that Dianne
was too thin by half and needed to eat something
substantial, if not to fatten her up, then at least to give her
brain food to keep her sharp for her first appointment with
her new employer. Dianne had struggled to eat it all: a large
bowl of porridge, topped with cream and sugar, followed by
a plate brimming to the edge with bacon, eggs and fried
tomato, a side plate with toast and a cup of hot tea.

But as to it being brain food, Dianne felt that she could
think of nothing but how full she felt.

"I won't have all of Carlton saying I wouldn't feed you
properly." Mrs Todd had said. "Now eat up and don't make
a fuss!"

And so she'd made a valiant attempt to eat as much as
possible, because she hadn't wanted to offend her landlady
on her first morning, but decided that she would have to
speak firmly to her for the future. She would have to *make*
her understand, because she would make herself sick if she
tried to keep this up.

As the Todds' front garden gate swung shut after her,
Dianne's attention switched from having overeaten to the fact
that she was approaching the schoolhouse. The daylight
afforded her a clearer and more detailed view of the small

town into which she had come the previous night. The school was a rather grand building in comparison with most of the other modest cottages and houses. It had a high pitched roof that slanted down either side, and huge cement steps at the front that brought the students and staff to the front porch.

The residence next door was not quite as grand, but was built with the same stone and roofed with the same iron. It was very much part of the school building.

Since it was a Saturday, there were no children arriving ready for school. It was just as she had arranged, so that she could have a couple of days to settle before she began to teach in class. Apprehension was tugging at her, with butterflies in her stomach and still just a hint of dread. Dianne could not completely dismiss all she'd heard about the schoolmaster, and he hadn't done anything to dispel these rumours in his unfriendly greeting the previous night. Mary-Ann had wanted to tell her a deep dark secret about him, but Peter had prevented her, saying that it was only hearsay, and that he didn't think it was worth repeating. Still, to sum up, he was arrogant, aloof, unfriendly and generally cross.

So Dianne didn't know why she should be startled to hear the deep, authoritative voice addressing her the moment she'd set foot inside the classroom door. It fitted Mary-Ann's description perfectly.

"I do hope your husband will not be making a practice of this," the stern-faced schoolmaster barked. "It's not acceptable to be sending one's wife with excuses for lateness. Tardiness will not be tolerated with students or staff alike. I trust you will convey my message to your husband, Mrs. Pierceson."

Dianne knew at once that Mr Schrouder had believed her application was from a man, and that was why he had accepted her for the position.

"My husband is dead, sir."

The words rushed from her lips, as she dared to look into the face of this awe-inspiring man. For just a few seconds Dianne saw a look of sympathy, and it was in that brief moment that she saw something that challenged her preconceived notion of the man. She had already judged him to be a cold, unfeeling bitter old man, but that brief glimpse revealed his youth. She was caught completely off guard. Mr. Schrouder, Carlton Schoolmaster, was not middle-aged or elderly, and though on the whole he presented himself as a hard and authoritative man, she wondered if she had really seen compassion in his expression. But if she had, it had only been for an instant. When she looked again the mask of unfeeling indifference was again in place.

"I offer you condolences, Mrs. Pierceson," Mr. Schrouder said as by rote, "but I fail to see why you haven't simply written and informed me of this sudden tragedy. There was no need for *you* to come all this way to let me know he can no longer fill the position."

Dianne dropped her eyes and shifted her feet nervously. Richard Schrouder had misinterpreted who she really was and was most certainly under the impression that it would be Mr. Samuel Pierceson who would be his co-worker. It was becoming quite apparent that he would never have invited a woman to fill this position, no matter how qualified nor how desperate.

"I'm sorry that you have misunderstood, Mr. Schrouder." Dianne began her explanation while trying to resurrect her fading confidence. "You see, I was the one who applied and was accepted by yourself as the assistant teacher at Carlton public school. *Mrs* Samuel Pierceson."

Tension hung in the air for a few moments. Dianne watched his face for a reaction, but when it came, it was much stronger than any she could have imagined.

"I do not employ women, Mrs. Pierceson," he spoke sharply. "Your place is in the home looking after your husband and family. It would seem that you have deliberately attempted to deceive me into giving you a position. I refuse to accept it. Do you understand?"

"But, my husband is dead, and I have no family or home," Dianne defended herself fiercely. "I have no money to buy food or clothes. This job is my last hope. I haven't any other options open to me. You must see that I am desperate for employment." Her confident approach had definitely lost its starch and she sounded almost as if she were pleading.

"You can save your emotional display, madam. It won't carry any weight with me." His words were cold and calculated. "I've told you that I do not, and will not, employ a woman. You might just as well take the next train back to where you came from."

Dianne wiped angrily at a lone tear that had betrayed her attempt to appear calm and professional.

"Mr. Schrouder," she finally spoke, having regained some self control, "whatever your opinions of a woman's role, I am demanding that you give me a chance to prove my worth to you."

"Demanding?" he interrupted with one eyebrow raised.

"I have no option but to work here because without a wage I simply can't exist. And you don't have any choice," she hurried on. "It will take months to find another applicant as qualified and capable as myself." She stared unflinchingly at her prospective employer, sure that to hold his gaze would be a proof of her determination. It was a silent battle of the wills, neither one prepared to back down.

"You are correct, Mrs. Pierceson," Richard Schrouder eventually conceded, still maintaining his stern stare. "I have no choice but to start you with the classes in two days time, but I am adamant when I say that you will not stay. As soon as a suitable *male* replacement has been found, you will be free to look for a husband and home."

Dianne ended the interview quickly before she lost complete control and flew at the man and laid into him. He was not only unnerving but positively disagreeable. Mary-Ann Todd's assessment seemed more and more credible.

Dianne walked aimlessly away from the school grounds, her mind in turmoil as she busily tried to justify the situation. It wasn't until she had reached the outskirts of the town that she pulled her emotions and logic together again.

Well, at least I get to start, she consoled herself. *Surely he's not so unreasonable as to deny me the work if I prove that I'm capable.* With these thoughts in mind, she turned back towards Mrs. Todd's boarding house.

Chapter Three

"It's time you either found a job or a new man!" Those had been the words that had forced this decision in the first place. Of course Dianne had known that it had been brewing ever since she'd gone to live with her parents-in-law, but finally hearing it expressed out loud had caused her to reel, nevertheless. She would never have come in the first place if there had been any other alternative. But there hadn't been, and at the time she'd been in such a state of despair that she'd hardly known what to do.

When she'd first been told that her husband had been killed in an accident she hadn't been able to think about anything at all. During those first few weeks following the tragedy she had been in a daze, not even able to consider how she might support herself. It wasn't until a member of the parish council had come to the door and announced that she could no longer live in the manse - that a new minister would be moving in and she would have to make other arrangements - that she'd stopped to consider her living arrangements at all.

As a young bride, Dianne Pierceson had never stopped to wonder what would happen if anything were to happen to her husband Samuel, and he had only been twenty-eight years old. It wasn't as if they'd expected anything to happen.

Ever since he'd graduated from seminary, and had received his first appointment, Dianne and Samuel had felt happy and secure in the manse provided for them by the church.

The only choice left open to Dianne following the funeral was to go and live with Samuel's parents, the senior Reverend James Pierceson and his wife. Dianne's own mother had remarried after her father had died, and they had returned to England shortly after Dianne had married. Dianne's new step-father was not interested in his wife's adult daughter, and since he was also a stern, controlling man, he never gave Dianne's mother the option of being any help to her grieving daughter.

So the Reverend James Pierceson and his wife had taken Dianne in. The senior reverend had been more like his son - open, caring and at times cheerful, but Samuel's mother was a bitter woman, and always had been as far as Dianne had known, and Ruth Pierceson had never made any secret about the fact that she had never thought Dianne good enough for her son. This attitude had only been aggravated by the period of time that Dianne had labelled her own barrenness.

Dianne and Samuel had married young, as soon as he'd finished seminary, and had joyfully anticipated the arrival of children, but no child ever arrived. Samuel had been very philosophical about it. He'd said that it was all in God's hands, and that while it was just the two of them, they would apply themselves to God's work with all their might, and celebrate the child when it came.

But Samuel's mother had made many snide remarks on the topic, and didn't try to hide the fact that she felt it was Dianne's fault that they had provided no grandchildren. Dianne had tried not to let her mother-in-law's bitter spirit crush her. Samuel had been wonderful during this time.

He'd known his mother's nasty tongue, and had always supported his wife during the hard times.

But then suddenly Samuel was gone, and Dianne found herself dependent on his parents.

"It's time you either found a job or a new man!"

Ruth's callous pronouncement had been hard to hear, but had at least forced Dianne to do something. She had known she would not be able to stay. Ruth had wanted Dianne to take off her wedding ring in the hope of luring a new husband, but Dianne had been unable even to bear such an idea. The only other option had been for her to seek work to support herself, and in the difficult times which had the whole country struggling, it had been a very difficult task. Jobs were scarce for men, and there was little being offered for a woman. But Ruth's broad hints continued. Dianne was not ignorant of how the tithes in the collection plate had dwindled, and she knew that she was not just an emotional burden, but a financial one also. Not that the Reverend James would ever say so, but Ruth Pierceson had no scruples about saying it outright.

The couple of times Dianne had seen work advertised, it was for menial domestic work. She had applied, but found herself unsuccessful. Ruth had found yet another reason to make her feel guilty, accusing her of thinking herself too good for such work just because she had an education.

So when the Reverend James had shown her the advertisement for a teacher in a small country school, she had taken the chance. At first she had thought it a waste of time, since the advertisement had clearly stated 'only males need apply', but her father-in-law had encouraged her to try anyway. She had the qualifications, and he had reasoned that she would lose nothing by trying.

Dianne had taken the advice, and written the letter. After she'd signed it she noticed that the Mrs was looking decidedly like a Mr, the 's' being poorly formed, but she decided to leave it. Mrs Samuel Pierceson, it read. It was Mrs Samuel Pierceson who had made the decision to take charge of her life, to pick up what had been left for her and make good for herself.

But now, as she sat in the spare room of a woman she had only just met, trying to phrase exactly how she would explain to her new employer why he ought to employ her despite the fact that she was a woman, for the first time, she felt terrified. Mr Schrouder was no worse than the threat of poverty and loneliness, but for some reason, he was the first person Dianne had allowed to affect her; and she was intimidated.

Chapter Four

P eter and Mary-Ann Todd had congratulated Dianne on the fact that she was to start her new job on Monday morning, despite the mistaken identity. Mary-Ann was particularly pleased that Dianne had bearded the lion in his den, so to speak, and stood up for herself. Peter only smiled at this and muttered something along the lines that he was certain that Richard Schrouder wasn't that bad.

Sunday morning dawned and the Todds invited Dianne to attend church with them. She had lost track of time in all the tumult of the past two days, but quickly agreed to join them. As she had been a minister's wife for six years, she was quite used to Sunday service, and was in fact glad of the opportunity to go to worship and pray.

There was only one moment as she dressed for church, when she caught sight of her reflection in the mirror, that she remembered Samuel. She knew she couldn't be bent over with grief forever, and in fact had decided that it was time to get on with living, but she couldn't help the ache she felt. He had always been so encouraging when she'd prepared to go out, and had always told her how wonderful she looked. It was only for a moment that the sadness surfaced, but she knew she couldn't sink down into it again. She had to look up and go forward from now on.

Dianne was surprised to learn that the Todds usually walked to most places they needed to go, including the church, even though they had an old Model T Ford.

"These are hard times," Peter Todd had said when Dianne asked about the old car she'd seen parked in the shed out the back of the house. "We save the old girl for long distances and emergencies."

Dianne didn't have to be told about hard times, though she and Samuel had never owned a car while tram cars and trollies were within easy reach. But she had never realised that petrol was yet another thing that had to be rationed in the face of the disastrous economic collapse.

The little church was about half a mile further along the main street from the Todds' house and the morning walk was pleasant, giving Dianne an opportunity to take a proper look at the town.

"I'm sure everyone will be glad to meet you, Mrs. Pierceson," Peter Todd spoke up above the sound of the crunching gravel underfoot, "although, I daresay many of them will be surprised to see it's a *Mrs.* Pierceson who will be teaching their children and not a Mr. Pierceson."

Dianne turned towards him, wearing a puzzled frown. "Hasn't there ever been a female teacher at Carlton?" she asked.

"Not since Mr. Richard Schrouder has been the master," Mary-Ann sniffed contemptuously. "He's a very strange man!"

"Now Mother," Peter said in a patient tone, "it's not very Christian to speak ill of others."

"Then it's not Christian to speak of Mr. Schrouder at all," she retorted, unrepentant, "I'm sure no-one has anything good to say about the man."

"If he's such a disreputable character, I wonder that the

parents don't withdraw their children from the school and demand his resignation," Dianne observed.

"Now, now, Mrs. Pierceson." Peter spoke as if to smooth troubled waters. "Despite my wife's obvious dislike of the man, there has never been any evidence to prove he's anything other than honest and hardworking. You'll never see him in a hotel or any public place engaging in strong drink, nor will you ever see him in a place where there is questionable behaviour."

"You'll never see him in church either!" Mary-Ann argued.

Dianne cast her eyes from one to the other as they disagreed openly.

"He always used to go...before," Peter carefully defended the schoolmaster's position.

"Before what?" Dianne's curiosity had been aroused, and she suddenly had an urge to find out as much as she could about her new employer. But her question remained unanswered as they had arrived at their destination, and Peter Todd led his wife and new boarder up the stone steps into the place of worship.

Dianne enjoyed the Sunday morning church service. Over the years of being part of a minister's family, she had seen all sorts of men behind the pulpit, and not all of them were as enthusiastic and engaging as this man, the Reverend Jonathon Andrews. While on other occasions she had heard sermons that were dull and uninteresting, this morning, she was comforted to hear a minister speak with almost as much conviction as her Samuel had displayed over the years.

When the benediction had been given, and Mr Andrews had walked back to the door, Dianne prepared herself to meet new people, townspeople who would be curious about the new teacher. She stood up from the pew and joined the line of people in the aisle who were moving slowly past the minister, each one shaking his hand in greeting as they left the church. When it was Dianne's turn she returned the smile of the middle-aged man.

"You must be the new school teacher," he said in a warm friendly tone. "My name is Jonathon Andrews."

"Dianne Pierceson," she returned.

"Welcome to Carlton, Miss Pierceson."

"Mrs Pierceson," Dianne corrected politely. "I am a widow."

"I'm very sorry to hear that," he said with genuine sympathy in his tone. "I am very pleased to see that we now have a lady teacher," he continued, taking a few extra moments to talk to her. "I'm sure the little ones will adjust much more quickly with a motherly figure at their school."

"Thank you, Mr Andrews." Dianne responded with a wide smile. "I hope I can meet everyone's expectations."

At that point, the minister leaned closer to her and lowered his voice, obviously wanting to keep his next comments for her ears only. "Our schoolmaster is a very hurt and lonely young man, Mrs. Pierceson. Don't mind his apparent indifference. What he really needs is friends who care." Having said this he turned away from her to greet the next parishioner.

Dianne moved out into the porch and down the steps to the crowd gathering outside. She was puzzled by the strange passing comment, and began to wonder if she'd even heard it at all, or if perhaps she had just imagined it.

Peter Todd took it upon himself to introduce her to the different families as the new schoolteacher, but Dianne could hardly remember one face or name from another, but she smiled and shook hands with everyone she met. She hoped that she was making the right impression, as her thoughts were somewhat distracted by what the minister had said to her about the schoolmaster. She had seen rudeness, arrogance, even indifference, but she didn't know how to match that with what the minister had told her about him.

"Forgive me, Mrs. Pierceson." Mary-Ann Todd's voice broke into her thoughts as they strolled back toward home. "I hope you don't mind me saying, but you seem very distant, dear. Did the service upset you at all?"

"No! Oh no, Mrs. Todd." Dianne was quick to reassure her. "I was just thinking about tomorrow. You know - a new job and all that goes with it."

The older woman seemed satisfied by the explanation. "I guess there are a lot of things you will need to prepare before starting off tomorrow."

It was at this point that Dianne realised that she had been so focussed on the mix up with her arrival, and the confrontation concerning her position that she had completely forgotten to take the extra time to find out from the schoolmaster his expectations and outline the details of her class.

"I will be out all afternoon, Mrs. Todd," Dianne suddenly blurted. "There's still a lot of things I need to get organised."

"On a Sunday?" Peter Todd gave a disapproving frown.

"Normally I wouldn't think of working on a Sunday, but I've just realised I am not at all prepared, and I really must make a good impression on my first day."

"Well, I'd save your strength, my dear," Mary-Ann Todd said. "That man won't be won over by a good impression, so long as it's a woman who's making it."

Dianne remained quiet for a while longer as they continued on their way, mulling over in her mind all of the opinions and comments that had been expressed about the schoolmaster.

"Mrs. Todd." she finally summoned courage to speak the question troubling her. "What is it about Mr. Schrouder that makes him so antagonistic toward women?"

"Huh!" Mary-Ann laughed out loud. "Wouldn't we all like to know. I just wonder how it was he ever married in the first place."

"Married!" Dianne sounded shocked. "I didn't know there was a Mrs. Schrouder."

"Well, it's no wonder at that," the older woman continued sounding self-satisfied.

"Now, mother," Peter warned using a low tone.

"Well, no-one has caught sight of her in years," she went on ignoring her husband's signal. "Some people say he's gone and knocked her off."

"Mary-Ann!" This time, Peter raised his voice in rebuke.

"Well, you know that's what people say," she said defensively.

"Not all," he answered, firmly.

"True! The other half say she ran off with a travelling salesman!"

Dianne's mouth fell open as she heard and processed the common gossip which was tragic in either case.

"Don't pay any mind to what's said!" Peter Todd turned to Dianne and saw that she was shocked by what had been said. "The fact is, no-one really knows what happened to Mrs. Schrouder or the baby."

"Baby?" Dianne continued in amazement.

"You may as well tell her the whole story, now you've begun," Mary-Ann Todd urged her husband. "You're the one who seems to know all the facts."

"Richard Schrouder shifted here to Carlton ten or eleven years ago," Peter Todd began in a subdued tone. "He came with his young wife who was in the family way at the time. They seemed like a nice young couple - friendly and helpful - in fact, he was the one who worked really hard to upgrade the standard of education here. If there's one thing nobody can fault, it's his dedication to the school." He paused briefly to glare at his wife as if to dare her to disagree. "When the baby arrived, he seemed happy and as proud as any of the young fathers in the town."

"And he used to go to church?" Dianne asked, trying to fit all the pieces together.

"Regularly," Peter Todd replied. "He even offered to help set up a Sunday School for the children."

"Yes, but where is he now?" Mary-Ann seemed determined to prove her side of the story.

Peter Todd noticed the look of confusion on Dianne's face. "Nobody really knows what happened, Mrs. Pierceson." He paused and sighed deeply. "Something went wrong, we know that much, but as to what exactly, no-one can say for sure."

"But Mrs. Schrouder and the baby are gone?" Dianne asked intrigued.

"Can't even say that for certain. He never allows anybody inside his house, so no-one can really say whether they are there or not."

The conversation ended at this point as the small group came upon the gate that opened into the Todds' front garden. But Dianne had a million thoughts buzzing around in her mind from everything she'd heard.

Chapter Five

When Dianne crossed to the school that afternoon, she decided to take the humble approach and offer an apology for her previous rudeness. When it seemed that the schoolmaster had accepted this, she then asked him to give her an exact outline of what he expected of her in this position. Richard Schrouder, with firm set face, nodded curtly and silently handed Dianne a well prepared list of responsibilities and expectations. She had watched his countenance carefully for any sign of human feeling as she had spoken. She had noted his face was undeniably young and strangely handsome, yet devoid of emotion. She left the brief interview puzzled. Her curiosity had been well and truly aroused by all the things she'd learned that morning. She couldn't help but wonder about his wife and child. The gossip Mrs Todd had repeated was too terrible, and Dianne couldn't help thinking about it, hoping that it was just nasty rumours, but unable to dismiss it based on the evidence she saw with her own eyes. Her afternoon's work was severely hampered now by all her wandering thoughts.

Monday morning dawned, and Dianne leapt from her bed, her body buzzing with nervous energy. Today would be the first day of her teaching career. The time she had spent studying as a girl just out of school was about to be put to good use. She was excited about meeting the children and working with them.

From the schoolmaster's list of instructions she had learned that, for the time being at least, she would be responsible for the complete education of the very young children from ages five to eight years old. Also on various occasions she would be called upon to take special classes with the whole school. It had crossed her mind to question Mr. Schrouder about the reasons why he had left her with a larger work load than his own, but her desire to impress and prove her worth prompted her to accept it without question.

After having tried without success, to finish the large breakfast that Mrs Todd insisted on preparing, Dianne took her coat and bag in hand, mumbled a hasty goodbye and set out into the cool autumn morning, walking briskly across to the school yard. The main school building had had an extension added to the far end some years previously, making way for an extra classroom and creating space for two teachers. This expansion had been prompted by an increase in enrolments following the introduction of compulsory education. The school board had become aware that one teacher could not possibly give equal and fair attention to such a wide variety of ages and different standards of work.

"Good morning, Mr. Schrouder," she called to the schoolmaster as she entered the school ground, the smile covering her features fuelled by the excitement she felt about her first day.

Richard Schrouder nodded in response, although his expression did not soften from the same firm set expression that she had seen every time she'd met with him.

"There will be an assembly every Monday morning, Mrs. Pierceson," he spoke evenly. "We gather to sing the National Anthem and salute the flag. I will introduce you to the students then."

He turned back to unlock the main schoolroom door, and Dianne walked the extra yards further to fit her own new key into the lock of the smaller classroom. A wave of pleasure flowed over her as she opened the door and stepped into her new classroom.

There were several desks set out, with benches for the students to use as seats. A blackboard was fixed to one wall, with new long sticks of chalk resting on its ledge, ready for use. A yard ruler, a map of Australia, and one of the world, a picture of the King and a chart with letters neatly printed on it, all sat tidily in their own designated position.

Dianne had only just set her own things down on the large desk when she heard the sound of the school bell. Stepping out into the fresh air she saw her employer standing near the flag pole ringing the brass bell mounted on a large frame. At first she thought he had that same indifferent expression that was becoming familiar, but as students began to assemble, she saw something about him that surprised her. He didn't actually smile, but a look came into his eyes that indicated he thought more of his pupils than perhaps he might normally let on. Dianne simply couldn't dismiss the things she'd heard. Was this man a fiend, with his wife and small child locked away from the rest of the world? At some moments she could believe it, but at other times, like now, watching him acknowledge the gathering students, she couldn't think of anything less likely. But then did one ever really know everything there was to know about another person?

She shook the intruding thoughts firmly from her mind, and determined to pay attention. It didn't take long for the entire student body to gather into uniform lines, graded in terms of height. It was quite obvious this was a drill they had practised many times before. There could not have been more than thirty children, but their order and efficiency impressed Dianne as she watched quietly. Even the tiny children stood quietly at attention and seemed to sing with equal enthusiasm as they watched the two older boys raise the flag.

Following the oath of allegiance, spoken in unison by the whole assembly, Richard Schrouder stepped forward to speak. "Mrs. Pierceson has joined us this morning. I expect you to give her the same respect and attention you have given me, even though she will not be with us for very long."

Up until that last sentence, Dianne had been on a high of anticipation, but as he reinforced his intention to dismiss her as quickly as possible she felt a stab of disappointment. It only took a few moments for her to gather her courage and determine to face the task and not be intimidated. She had the job for the time being, and she was sure she could prove her worth.

Dianne sighed heavily as the last child left the classroom. A weariness had descended upon her unlike any she'd ever experienced. She had been one week at the Carlton Public School. Actually being in the classroom, and staying mentally alert and active had been more taxing than she had ever thought possible during her training. Not that the children were particularly difficult to manage. Mr Schrouder had obviously set the standard of discipline, and other than a few minor mishaps with the very small children, on the whole they all behaved according to her instruction. She'd had to contend with the odd scraped knee, and a black eye that had been the result of a badly aimed ball during recess, but these things would not have been a trial to her at all if it hadn't been for the cloud of discouragement that had begun to settle on her spirit. She had expected to be tired, but she had somehow hoped that Richard Schrouder would soften towards her; show some encouragement, maybe even his approval of her work. But he had maintained his stiff, guarded attitude, and barely acknowledged her greetings, let alone offered a word of encouragement. It was terribly depressing on top of a week of mental and emotional drain.

She knew she should probably be reporting her progress to him but hesitated to do so. She was certain that he would pay little regard to her efforts, and she didn't think she could face any likely derogatory comments today.

She tried to take comfort in the fact that several parents had sent along notes of welcome and encouragement. These should have boosted her morale, but somehow, Dianne wanted Richard Schrouder's approval of her work. She rested her head in her hand, leaning her elbows on the desk and she sighed again. She was beginning to believe that perhaps her expectations were unreasonable in the current circumstances.

"Mrs. Pierceson!" Dianne looked up to see an older boy standing in the doorway of her class room. "Excuse me," he apologised, "but Mr. Schrouder has sent me to ask if you would come and see him. He wants to tell you something!"

Dianne gave the lad a weak smile and pushed herself to her feet. "What's your name?" She asked quietly.

"Jansen, Ma'm. Ted Jansen."

"Thank you, Ted," she said in acknowledgement. "I'll be right along, just as soon as I've packed up my books."

He smiled, happy to have delivered the message, and disappeared from the room. Dianne quickly gathered her things and yet again dug deep to summon her courage. Her usual optimism was being seriously taxed, and in its place she was finding an unwanted pessimism born of intimidation. She was almost certain that if he wanted to speak to her, it would only be to make some other derogatory comment about female teachers.

"Mrs. Pierceson!" Richard's voice seemed to resound around the high ceilings of the larger classroom. "I have observed the attitude and response of the students towards you this past week, and I must say it has been positive."

Dianne looked up quickly, taken aback by what she'd heard, when she had expected to hear the exact opposite. She searched his eyes for signs of sincerity.

"Positive?" she asked, as if uncertain of what he meant.

"The children seem to have taken to you, and one or two parents have sent comments about it to me."

Dianne couldn't help the smile that broke out on her lips. After all her experience of Richard Schrouder and his attitudes she had never expected him to be admitting that she had done a good job.

"I do thank you for your efforts," he continued evenly, "however I must caution you: don't become too attached to the children or the position. I still intend to find a male replacement."

Dianne dropped her eyes as her temporary pleasure evaporated and the previous fatigue set in again.

"I didn't promise you anything more, Mrs. Pierceson," he said rather defensively.

She nodded meekly and turned to leave the classroom.

Chapter Six

The weekend passed fairly quickly. Yet it was long enough for Dianne to recover from her discouragement. Time spent with the Todds and a trip to church served as a tonic for her strained emotions.

The people at church were friendly and warmly welcoming, and a few, who were parents of school children, were full of praise and encouragement.

"My little Suzanne was so much happier than she usually is during the school term," a beaming young mother commented. "She was always so intimidated by that other man!"

"The teacher before?" Dianne asked absent mindedly.

"Oh no, Mrs. Pierceson," the mother said quickly. "The Carlton school has been struggling with just the one teacher, for some time now."

"Oh!" Dianne was a little dumbfounded and felt unable to make comment. Yet again she was meeting people who had a decidedly negative opinion of the schoolmaster. To some degree she wanted to revel in these opinions which somehow justified her position. If it hadn't been for her previous years in the manse, forever trying to head gossip off before it caused damage, she might have been tempted to slip into the stream of uncharitable opinions, and could probably have added a few of her own.

But as it was, she chose the way of long schooled conviction, and struggled to hold her own tongue.

The Monday morning was quite cold as Dianne set out early for her second week of teaching. She supposed that several more weeks would see the necessity for her having to light a fire each day to warm the little class room.

As she approached the classroom, Dianne uttered a prayer, and repeated to herself a Scripture she had read only that morning.

"Cast your burden upon the Lord and He will sustain you: He will never allow the righteous to be shaken."

That was what she felt she needed. She wasn't absolutely sure about the righteous thing in the light of her recent battles, but she wanted to know that she was not facing this strange situation alone, and she certainly wanted to feel that she would not be shaken by it. So with this prayer uttered for courage she walked on, prepared to not be shaken by Richard Schrouder.

"Good morning, Mr. Schrouder," she called with cheerful determination when she saw him striding toward her. But the tall master gave only his usual terse reply, without looking up at her, and without stopping as would have been basic manners. He walked past, and went straight to unlock his classroom door. Suddenly, Dianne had had enough and a fiery indignation began to bubble up inside her. She stepped after him, a spark of anger flashing in her eyes.

"Mr. Schrouder, your lack of common decency is disgusting. I may not be a man, but I am doing my best, and whatever your misgivings about the arrangement there's no possible reason for you to be so rude and to display such a poor example to your students."

She turned quickly on her heels and stormed off to her own classroom, her breath coming quickly as the adrenaline from her outburst continued to pump around her body. She pulled the classroom door shut behind her and went immediately to her desk where she sat down and promptly began to cry.

If she had prayed that she would not be shaken, she now felt as if she had been positively blown over. She had never been so out of control before, and couldn't understand why this insufferable man and his terrible manners had set her off in such a display. Her reaction certainly wasn't what she'd been brought up to, and suddenly she felt rather foolish.

"Why does he have to be so…so horrid and totally difficult to get along with," she spoke out loud, as if there was someone there to hear her. "If it wasn't for the money, I know I'd leave!"

Several minutes passed as Dianne went through the encounter again in her mind. She supposed that this morning's episode had been merely the match to the tinder, and that all of the emotional buildup of leaving the city, and trying to find a place of acceptance in a new town had been waiting to explode. Now she felt rather sorry that she'd been so dramatic about it, and in front of Richard Schrouder who always seemed to be looking to find fault too.

She was jerked out of her self pity by a firm rapping at the classroom door. Tears still stood conspicuously in her eyes and there were still traces on her cheeks. She made a hurried attempt to wipe the evidence from her face, hoping to hide the fact that she had been crying.

"Come in," she called, her voice not as stable as she would have liked.

The door opened and Dianne stared in total amazement. For the first time during her employment, the principal entered her classroom.

"Mrs Pierceson?" He spoke clearly, and yet Dianne could detect that his tone was definitely softer than ever she'd heard before. She suddenly recovered herself when it became apparent that he had been awaiting her permission to continue. She had been staring open-mouthed at the unique sight of him standing there.

"I'm sorry, Mr. Schrouder." She stumbled over her words. "I'm listening."

"I must apologise for my seemingly rude and unfriendly behaviour."

Dianne continued to stare in mute amazement, as she fully expected an explanation to follow. But no explanation came, and just as quickly as he had appeared he made his exit.

For some minutes following the encounter, Dianne remained in a state of shock. The whole experience, her violent outburst and his most unexpected apology, had quite muddled her thoughts.

"What a strange character," she muttered to herself as she eventually began to pull herself together. "I don't wonder that Mrs. Schrouder has disappeared. He must have been absolutely impossible to live with!"

Her musings were brought to an end as the sound of the school bell rang, calling everybody to assembly.

Chapter Seven

The assembly ran along the same lines as it had the previous week. The students stood in well formed lines, the anthem was sung and oath recited. The flag was raised, and there were only a few tense moments when the two boys in charge found a small knot in the cord. This almost threatened to upset proceedings, but luckily, it came undone without causing too much disruption.

There was a difference to the previous week however. Ted Jansen, whom Dianne recognised as the boy who'd delivered the message to her on Friday, arrived late. He had with him a smaller boy who was displaying obvious signs of reluctance. Ted had hold of the smaller child's arm and was all but dragging him. The child was struggling and making some muted protests. At one point when Ted saw the eyes of the entire school body upon him, he let the boy's arm dangle free, at which point the smaller child immediately took his opportunity to try and escape. Ted quickly swung around after the boy.

"Kenny!" he hissed through his teeth. "If you don't come and line up smartly, I'll tell Dad."

The transformation in the boy's behaviour was dramatic. Kenny immediately stopped struggling against his brother and followed along behind him as meekly as a tame lamb, falling into his designated spot without any further fuss. By the size of the boy, Dianne judged that Kenny would be one of her students. She also tucked away the incident into a may-be-useful-later corner of her mind, suspecting that there might be something in the warning Ted had used to get his little brother to comply.

"Kenny Jansen has been away sick, Mrs. Pierceson."

Richard spoke to her, as she watched the brothers line up. She was startled from her thoughts by his explanation. He spoke to her so little that she hadn't been expecting it, but she did nod in acknowledgment. She might have said something by way of a courteous response, but after the earlier emotional upheaval she couldn't even think of anything intelligent to say. So she restricted her response to a nod.

Once all her students had marched from the assembly area and entered the classroom, Dianne greeted them and announced that she would now call the roll. In her one week's experience, this task had not presented any great difficulties. It had seemed to her as if the children sat eagerly waiting to hear their names called, and felt a thrill of pleasure in answering 'present'. And so the call began as it had the previous week, and without exception each child answered its name when called; until she reached the name that had been marked with five consecutive 'A's for absent the week before.

"Kenny Jansen," she called. No answer was made.

"Kenny Jansen," Dianne repeated, her pencil poised ready to mark the name. Still there was no reply and Dianne looked up. She knew that the boy had arrived but was suddenly afraid that he might have slipped away while her attention had been occupied elsewhere. But to her relief, Kenny Jansen was sitting in the second row, his eyes cast down, his hands clasped tightly in front of him.

"Kenny!" Dianne spoke directly to the silent child. He made no effort to look up or respond. Dianne glared at him, frustration beginning to rise. "Kenny, please look up when I speak to you."

Despite all the firmness and command Dianne had injected into her tone, the boy did not respond.

"Kenny's stupid," blurted out Jamie, one of the bigger boys. "He never talks in school."

Dianne gave what she hoped was a strong glare of disapproval at the outspoken Jamie. When he looked suitably sudued, she changed tack.

"What do you mean he never talks in school, Jamie?" Dianne asked.

"He won't answer Mr Schrouder either. I reckon he'll get the cuts like he usually does."

"We'll see if there might not be a better way, shall we?" Dianne spoke a little smugly as she imagined the overbearing, intimidating head master punishing the small child.

Dianne continued calling the rest of the names on the list, making up her mind as she did so to tackle the problem of the silent Kenny as soon as the opportunity arose.

"Please take out your readers, class." Dianne gave her instruction, determined to occupy the students' minds while she worked with Kenny. "Suzannah and Timmy, you may choose a picture book from the shelf and I want all of you to read quietly for the next fifteen minutes."

The children obediently moved to retrieve their readers from their various shelves and it wasn't long before the entire class, including Kenny, had an open book on the desk in front of them.

Dianne smiled inwardly as she watched their orderly compliance. This was the ideal that teaching staff were asked to maintain in the classrooms, should one of the school inspectors make a surprise visit. She had been terrified that she wouldn't be able to manage the children's behaviour, but she need not have worried. They were normal, laughing, shouting and mischievous at play time, but in the classroom they abided by the expectations that had been established. She would like to have attributed this reliable behaviour to the fact that they were a wonderful lot of children, but common sense told her it was the work of the schoolmaster. He had set the standard and had managed to teach them how to obey. And, she had to admit, that on the whole it was not a reign of terror. There were too many shenanigans outside the classroom for her to believe that.

But despite the success in most cases, Kenny Jansen was apparently an exception to the rule. By looking at the child, she couldn't imagine that it was defiance that was the problem. That he might indeed be 'stupid' or better put, simple, could also be a possibility, but Mr Schrouder hadn't warned her of any such problem, so she had to assume that it was bad behaviour, but for what reason she had no idea.

"Kenny!" Dianne spoke his name expecting him to respond, but he showed no sign that he'd even heard her. "Kenny," she repeated. "Please come to my desk."

Much to her chagrin, Kenny still made no sign that he had even heard her. Dianne stood up somewhat frustrated but by no means beaten, and walked over to stand next to the boy's desk. "Kenny," she insisted again. "If you do not respond when I speak to you, I will have to tell your father."

If she thought these 'magic' words that Ted had used earlier on his brother would bring the same compliance they had for Ted she was very much mistaken. Quite without warning, the small child slipped out of his seat and made a mad dash for the door, knocking over the waste paper basket as he went. There was a tittering amongst the rest of the students as they began to whisper their thoughts aloud.

"Thank you, class." Dianne spoke sternly. "Please return to *quiet* reading, as I've asked." They instantly complied, but she felt quite sure that certain ones of them were itching to make some comment. Her own thoughts were now quite taken up with the problem of Kenny Jansen. Making a quick decision, she began to follow the small boy out of the classroom door.

"Jamie," she called to her talkative student as she moved, "please go next door and have Mr Schrouder send Ted Jansen to me at once."

Jamie was quick to obey, and followed his new teacher out of the classroom door.

Once outside, Dianne scanned the area outside to see if she could see where Kenny had gone, but the few moments she'd taken to settle the class had been enough for the child to get away.

She guessed he must have run back home and was perplexed, if not a little annoyed that she had not been able to get the better of this tricky situation. She hoped that Mr Schrouder would not hear about it, as she felt that she couldn't bear his look of disapproval, for he would frown upon her female weakness for having failed to keep order in the situation.

But of course he would hear of it, she suddenly realised. Ted would tell him eventually, because he'd been called out of class.

As if her thoughts had conjured him up, Dianne's heart sank as she heard the stern tones of the schoolmaster as he strode across the schoolyard toward her.

"What is the problem, Mrs Pierceson?" he asked without any attempt to sound helpful or sympathetic.

"Kenny Jansen has run out of the classroom. I'd guess he's gone home," she said, sounding somewhat deflated.

"He won't have gone home." Dianne suddenly became

aware that Ted had come outside with his teacher. "He'll be hiding under the storage shed."

Richard immediately strode off in that direction, and Dianne noticed that he carried the long cane that normally stood in the corner behind his desk.

"Ted," she turned her anxious face toward the boy. "How do you know he hasn't gone home?"

"He'd never go home. Dad would beat the living daylights out of him."

"Well, why has he run off and hid from me. He wasn't in any serious trouble. I wasn't going to punish him."

"No, but he'll get the cuts from Mr Schrouder. He always does, and then he'll get it when he gets home anyway."

"Ted!" Dianne's tone had risen in intensity. "Please tell me what you are talking about. I simply don't understand why Kenny has run off like this, nor why he should be getting beaten at all!"

"Mr Schrouder gives him the cane because…you know…like when we muck about."

"Ted!" Dianne wasn't getting the answers she was looking for. "Kenny wasn't mucking about. He simply wouldn't answer me."

"He never does," Ted offered.

"What do you mean?" Dianne asked.

"I don't know Mrs Pierceson. Just Kenny knows he's going to get it, but he's like a scared rabbit, and that only makes it worse."

"You mean Mr Schrouder beats him worse."

"Not Mr Schrouder." Ted dropped his eyes as if he didn't want to say anything else.

"Who then? Does he think I'm going to beat him?"

"No…" Ted was being quite hesitant. "He's scared of our dad."

Suddenly Dianne thought she understood. She wasn't certain, of course, but she thought she knew enough. If her guess was correct, Kenny and Ted's father used his belt a bit too freely and had managed to terrorise his younger son. Along with that, Richard Schrouder, who probably thought he was administering the normal punishment for mis-behaviour was in fact aggravating a very complex situation. Dianne turned from Ted and began to walk briskly in the direction the schoolmaster had gone.

"Go back to class, Ted," she called over her shoulder. "I will handle this situation now."

By the time Dianne came to where Kenny was hiding beneath the store shed which was raised up on stumps, she was possessed of a fiery courage. She had heard her employer command that the child come out, and she watched as the little boy crawled out looking just like the scared rabbit that Ted had described.

"Kenny." The schoolmaster spoke firmly. "You know that you must not disobey your teacher, and that when you do, you must take the punishment."

Kenny made no move, only stood with his head down, and his small body trembling.

"Excuse me, Mr Schrouder," Dianne broke into the scene. "May we talk for a moment?"

Richard cast a look of annoyance in her direction. "I will speak with you in a few moments, Mrs Pierceson. Please wait for me in your classroom."

Dianne was almost tempted to turn back to do as she was asked, but the look of Kenny Jansen was so pathetic, she simply couldn't leave the situation as it was.

"No! This cannot wait." She used every ounce of courage she could find, and fixed what she hoped was a look of determination on her face as she dared to overrule her superior. "Go back to you seat, Kenny. At once!" She barked at him, her voice choked with anxiety sounding strangely harsh.

Kenny didn't wait for a second chance at reprieve, but scrambled away toward the classroom. Dianne bravely watched Richard's face turn different shades of red, determined that she would not back down.

"What is the meaning of this outrageous display of insubordination?" His normally deep steady voice was broken by the shock and anger that had overtaken him. "How dare you undermine my authority in this way!"

"Please, Mr Schrouder." Dianne had lost her starch and was all but pleading. "There are many things that we should discuss before you go on in this manner."

"There is nothing that I need to discuss with you!" he said unkindly. "Such an act of insubordination is absolutely unforgivable." He turned and began to stride back toward his own room, leaving Dianne to stare, open-mouthed after him. For a few seconds she thought she would just let him go but a conviction suddenly descended upon her. Eventually her weak knees obeyed her command to follow the man.

"Mr Schrouder! Wait!" She called after him, but still angered he continued on without even showing a sign that he'd heard her. Dianne broke into a run in an effort to catch him, and was soon by his side, puffing from both the physical exertion and the heightened emotion. "Please, just listen." She puffed as she kept walking just to keep up with him. Richard showed no intention of relenting, and before she had time to realise where her indignation had taken her, she had reached out and taken hold of his arm, pulling him to an ungraceful halt. "Listen to me!" She almost shouted at him this time. "That little boy is suffering from an intense fear of being beaten, and your *punishments* are making it ten times worse! I'm not a psychiatrist, but it doesn't take much to see that Kenny Jansen is not reacting as a normal well-balanced child should. From what Ted has reluctantly told me, there seems to be something going on at home. I believe their father is probably being too rough with them – I mean beating them. Did you know that?" She broke off her tirade, her face flushed and her breath coming in quick gasps. She waited, suddenly wondering what on earth had possessed her to challenge such an austere figure of authority. She could almost imagine herself packing up her bags and leaving already, but she held his gaze, looking for his response.

"If you would kindly let go of my arm, Mrs Pierceson." He eventually broke the emotion-charged silence, and brought Dianne to the realisation that she had not only assaulted the man verbally, she had a good grip on him physically as well. The blood rose in her face and she had the grace to feel embarrassed.

"I'm sorry," she stammered, "but I have to make you understand…"

"What do you mean his father beats him? Are you sure?" For the first time in their acquaintance, Dianne heard Richard's tone mellow considerably.

"I'm not sure, but from what Ted let slip, and from the way Kenny reacts, that would be my best guess. I hope I'm wrong, but I don't think I am."

Richard's brow furrowed with obvious concern, but he didn't say anything.

"I don't wish to interfere with your methods of discipline, sir," she explained. "I know how important it is, and can see just how high a standard of good behaviour has been achieved, but in this case…" She paused, overcome by what she'd observed in the little boy. "If the child is being beaten badly at home, this looks to be a case of abject fear and terror. I'm worried that further punishment here is really hurting the child."

Richard's eyes took on a far away look as he lifted his hand and pinched his thumb and forefingers together in the middle of his forehead. It was obvious that he had drifted into deep thought.

"What do you think we should do?" He asked, with no hint of harshness or annoyance in his tone.

"We should try to talk to him," Dianne offered tentatively. "We need to try and help him see that we are not going to beat him, but that we care about him, and want to help him learn. We need to teach him that he can trust us."

A silence hung in the air between them, as Dianne's words began to sink in. Eventually, Richard sighed, revealing a depth of despondency that Dianne had never seen in this man before.

"We'd best get back to the children, Mrs Pierceson," Richard said, but without any of his former tone of authority. "Detain Kenny at the recess time and we will try to talk with him." He delivered this instruction and then turned and walked up the steps and into his classroom.

As Dianne watched him go inside she was puzzled by the whole encounter. Richard Schrouder was a complex individual himself, and right at that moment, the gossip about him just didn't seem to fit.

Chapter Eight

Despite all good intentions, Kenny's reaction was as before, as if fuelled by an unreasoning terror. She was not quite certain that Kenny might not actually have some sort of mental disorder as his symptoms seemed to display, but for the time being, she had subscribed to this other theory, and would watch carefully to see just how it would work out. Whatever the cause, Dianne was deeply troubled as she watched the small child freeze up. She didn't dare mention anything in reference to his father, nor did she mention the schoolmaster.

The other children had gone outside to play, and while Dianne had asked Kenny to remain, she felt that he was on the edge of bolting at any moment.

"Kenny, would you like me to read you a story?" Dianne had no concept of what she could or should do, and grasped at this idea as a last resort. Kenny made no response to her offer, but Dianne picked up a story book anyway. There was no other option available that she could think of in the tension of the moment.

Sliding into the very low bench seat next to her student, Dianne opened the book on the desk. She made every effort to ignore his state of frozen indifference: the fact that he did not look at her or acknowledge her in any way.

"The Little Red Engine." Dianne read the title of the story, injecting as much enthusiasm and interest in her tone as she could. "I wish I could be like all the other engines," Dianne began to read the story. She went on, page after page, pointing out the illustrations that accompanied the story. She tried to concentrate on communicating the essence of the little engine's struggle, all the time realising that they were facing a much larger struggle of their own. To an observer, it would have appeared that Kenny didn't hear a word of the story. He made no response that he was even listening at all, and he never so much as glanced at the pictures that Dianne pointed out.

Finally, the story was finished, and Dianne held back the desire to let out a breath of frustration.

"I hope we can read another story tomorrow," Dianne said, trying to hide the despair from her tone. "You may go outside and play now."

Kenny didn't wait another second, but got up and quickly moved outside. As Dianne watched him go, she saw that Richard was standing just inside the doorway. She waited until Kenny was completely outside before she spoke.

"I didn't know what else to do," she said, this time letting her feelings show in her tone. "I didn't know you were there, or I would have made him wait to speak to you."

"I was here for most of the story," Richard said evenly, "and I doubt there would have been anything I could have done, that you did not already try."

"What do you mean?" Dianne was bewildered by this statement.

"I mean perhaps I have made a grave mistake, and now I don't know what I can do about it."

"You agree that by giving Kenny the cane when he disobeys might be making the situation worse?"

"I rarely have to use the cane, Mrs Pierceson. The children know what is expected of them, and on the whole they are obedient and compliant. I thought Kenny was just being deliberately difficult and defiant. I can't understand why I didn't see what you saw from the first."

Richard's tone sounded so hopeless that Dianne actually felt sorry for him. But she didn't have any answers to his dilemma.

"Do you think we should talk to his parents about his behaviour?" she asked, grasping at straws.

"Ordinarily, of course. But the fact is, I've always sent a letter home whenever I've administered any punishment. But if what you suspect is true, perhaps that is only stirring his father up."

Dianne had nothing else to offer.

"I think I will have to leave the situation in your hands for a few days," Richard said suddenly. "You will have to do what you think is best, and we will assess it next week, to see if there has been any improvement."

Dianne experienced a wave of mixed emotions. On the one hand she felt that Richard Schrouder had finally accepted her as an equal in education and management of children, and this bolstered her courage greatly. But when she considered what he had asked her to do, she nearly panicked. From what she had seen, Kenny Jansen appeared to be a complex and difficult child, probably the result of some extenuating circumstances. Nobody had seemed surprised by the way he had acted in her first class. All the children appeared to have accepted that Kenny's difficulty was normal behaviour for him. But Dianne knew it wasn't normal, and worried now whether she really did know best. She had been trained in basic classroom procedure, in how to teach children to read, write and do their sums. If Kenny's problem was due to some form of retardation or even if she had guessed correctly and it was due to a harsh hand at home, it was a psychological issue, and she didn't really have any idea of what was the right thing to do.

Chapter Nine

Despite the challenge that Kenny Jansen brought, Dianne continued to find delight in school teaching.

She pressed on the only way she knew how with Kenny, treating him as if he really had responded in the manner expected, talking to him in a friendly and encouraging manner. Gradually, she noticed that he seemed a little less tense, and several times she was thrilled to see him follow the writing task she had set for the other two beginners, taking his chalk to his slate and trying to form letters. He was quite behind the others, but she decided not to make any issue of it at all.

She had spoken sternly to any of the older children who used the word 'stupid' when referring to Kenny. Jamie had found himself detained after school on several occasions, and given the job of cleaning the chalk board and emptying the rubbish bin because he'd been unable to refrain from using the nasty adjective.

But on the whole, Dianne had found that there was little about her class that was beyond her. She was growing to love the children and really enjoyed knowing that what she taught them was actually helping them to improve in their reading, writing and arithmetic. She found it very fulfilling.

Richard had not really changed toward Dianne, in the sense that he was still stern and didn't make any effort at friendliness. He still maintained only a cool formal greeting. But at the end of each week, he did ask for a report on Kenny's progress. Dianne knew that he had made the extra efforts to try and encourage Kenny when he'd seen him in the school yard. It wasn't that there were any dramatic improvements, but there were signs of things being much better than they had been.

"I think you were right," Richard said to Dianne, after she'd delivered one of her reports on Kenny. "Before we can do anything else with the boy we will have to earn his trust!"

Dianne coloured slightly as she recognised the closest thing she'd ever heard to a compliment from his lips, and there was even an implied apology, when she thought about it.

"He actually admitted that I was right," she voiced her amazement to the Todds at dinner. "Ever since the business with Kenny Jansen, he has actually spoken to me as if I may actually know what I'm doing!"

"Well, I'm glad to hear that you're beginning to get along," Peter said, sounding satisfied.

"I wouldn't go that far, Mr. Todd," Dianne corrected. "I mean, he still doesn't smile or go out of his way to be friendly, but he is now at least civil and seems to listen."

"Humph! Well, I wouldn't get my heart set on too much more, my dear," Mary-Ann commented. "Just think of what his poor little wife must endure, if she's still alive, locked up in that house, never allowed out to see anybody at all!"

Dianne did think of the poor little wife. Often. Whenever she walked past the gate that connected the schoolgrounds to his back garden she wondered. She would crane her neck, trying to see if there was ever anybody hanging washing on the line, or picking fruit from one of the trees, and though she sometimes saw the actual wash flapping in the breeze, she had never seen anybody there putting it out or bringing it in. Curiosity was perhaps one of her weak points. It took a lot of will power not to just go through the gate and knock on the back door. But Dianne had heard some of the children whisper to each other about staying away from Mr Schrouder's house, or they'd cop it. Coupled with some of the town rumours – that he'd driven her mad and she was locked away; or that he'd killed her and hidden her body behind the woodpile – she hesitated. Of course, from what she had learned of the man from working with him, she seriously doubted that any of those rumours could possibly be true, but her other weak point was her overactive imagination. So wonder was all she did.

Despite Mrs. Todd's continuing disapproval of the Carlton Public School's master and her lingering curiosity, Dianne couldn't help but feel that she had gained ground. She had been installed in the job for nearly two months now, and there had been no more talk of a replacement, nor of the search for one, nor yet the imminent arrival of one. Dianne began to relax, feeling more secure in her position.

One particularly grey rainy morning, Dianne was greeted by the excited chatter of her students, already seated in the classroom due to the cold and damp outside.

"Did you see it, Mrs. Pierceson?" Timmy asked, his eyes wild with enthusiasm.

"See what, Timmy?" she calmly replied.

"All that rain has brought the creek down." Jamie was quick to offer the information. "My dad says it's flowing faster than it normally does!"

"Creek?" Dianne looked perplexed as she pondered the information.

"Yes, you know, Mrs. Pierceson," one of the older girls coaxed. "Down at the bottom of our school yard!"

Dianne thought for a moment, and then it began to become clear in her mind. She had, on several occasions, noted the dry, rocky creek bed that carved its way through the trees near the boundary, but it had never occurred to her that it might ever contain water.

"It did rain a lot, last night," she admitted. "Do you mean to say that the dry creek bed now has water in it?"

The entire class laughed at their teacher's ignorance.

"'Course, Mrs. Pierceson." Jamie sounded smug. "It always comes down after a lot of rain!"

Dianne gave a subdued chuckle as she recognised that she had been caught out by her students. "Well, class," she spoke up, "you can see that your teacher doesn't know everything!" She paused a moment to let her statement sink in. "Why don't you children give *me* a lesson, this morning." At their puzzled stares, she hurried on. "Perhaps, if it stops raining later, you can all take me down to the creek's edge and we will have a look. Perhaps you may be able to teach me something about it!"

The children immediately broke into animated chatter, as smiles abounded and excitement began to mount. Dianne knew that now the suggestion had been made, there was no going back on her word. She quickly scanned the sky through the window, and she could already see that the weather was beginning to clear. Suddenly she hoped that the excursion was safe, as doubts about the wisdom of the venture kept popping into her mind.

Eventually, it was quite obvious that it had stopped raining, and so after having lined the children up into their neat and orderly rows, she pulled Jamie aside. "Is it safe to go down to see the water, Jamie?" she asked, trying to sound confident about her decision.

"Oh, yes! " Jamie assured her, "Dad always takes us to have a look at the creek when it has water. We went already this morning!"

Dianne sighed with relief, and indicated for Jamie to take his place in the line, and then directed the children out of the door, on their way to the bottom of the school yard.

The playing area behind the school buildings was marked by a fence around its perimeter, but there was a gate that led onto another piece of land. Dianne knew that this land was also school property, and that the fence was there to prevent the children from playing close to the creek. It was now flowing swiftly, but generally it was dry and harmless. She halted the children at the gate, and spoke to them in a cautious tone, warning them of all the possible dangers that could result from any unruly behaviour.

The young students all nodded their heads, eager to reassure their teacher. They had no intention of being sent back to the classroom because they wouldn't behave themselves. Dianne took them to within a few yards of the bank, and ordered them to remain. They could all see the fast flowing water, brown from the mud being churned up as it flowed, with streaks of white bubbly foam dancing along the surface. The air was alive with the sound of the splashing and gurgling and Dianne was just as enthralled with the sight as her small group of students.

Despite the intention to discuss and learn about the phenomenon of flowing water, Dianne found herself in awe of the sight, and completely forgot about making comment or asking questions. She had no fear of the water at all, as it didn't present any threat.

It was this lack of fear mixed with her own intense curiosity that prompted her to move closer to the edge to get a better look at the spectacle. Ordinarily, it would have been perfectly all right, but the particular piece of bank she chose to stand on was on the side of the water course where fast flowing water had been methodically eating away chunks of earth that should have otherwise been supporting her. Unaware of just how precarious her position was she took the opportunity to take in the magnificence of the scene. But it didn't last long. Without warning Dianne's sight-seeing was brought to an abrupt end as the soft, sodden soil beneath her feet gave way, and fell with her in to the rushing torrent.

Dianne didn't have time to jump back from the unstable ground before it collapsed, and was already in the cold water before she had realized her dilemma. She didn't hear the children scream with fright as they watched their teacher topple ungracefully into the water. All she could think of was self-preservation as she reached out in panic for a tree root, that was protruding from the steep bank. A prayer of thanks came spontaneously to her lips as she caught hold of the dirty, ragged root and she felt its sturdiness. The busy, swirling water tugged at her skirt as she clung desperately to the woody lifeline.

"Mrs. Pierceson!" Dianne heard Jamie's voice calling above the din. "Are you drowned?"

She smiled as she heard the innocent conclusion that the boy had drawn.

"Jamie!" She called with all her energy, hoping it was enough to carry her voice above the din of the flood. "Could you call Mr. Schrouder, Jamie!"

Dianne deliberately tried to hide any trace of fear from her tone, not wanting to panic the children unnecessarily, and she hoped that they had sense enough to call the schoolmaster quickly as her grip, though firm, was tiring her arms.

The thought of dropping completely into the water and going with it down stream to a place where the bank was lower, and there climbing out, had crossed her mind, but Dianne was not a confident swimmer and did not know if she could remain afloat in the unknown depth.

So it was that Richard Schrouder found Dianne Pierceson, clinging tightly to the root, her hair loose and stringy clinging to the sides of her face. He immediately ordered the children back indoors, and came forward to the remaining edge.

"Mrs Pierceson!" he said in his normal grim tone. "What on earth are you doing?"

He didn't wait for her to answer, not that she could have said anything sensible anyway, but knelt down, took off his jacket and threw it carelessly back toward the retreating children, and reached out over the edge toward her.

"Grab hold of my arm," he called out to her, though the instruction was needless. Dianne had already reached towards him in an effort to secure a grip. Having established a firm hold, she began to drag her feet from the whirling flow, bringing them up to find a footing in the eroded bank.

"I think my feet are steady now," she called up to him. "If you could give me a pull..."

Suddenly, the whole scenario seemed ridiculous to her, but she swallowed her pride, and concentrated her energy in assisting in her own rescue.

There was strength in Richard's back that she could feel as she began to climb out of the water, but to her dismay, just as she was about to take hold of the top of the bank, her footing gave way, and she felt herself falling backward.

Once again, the mishap happened too quickly to give her time to stop herself, and so she failed to release her grip on Richard's arm, successfully pulling him forward into the water.

This time, she landed on her back, and she found herself submerged beneath the water. She felt something land on top of her, forcing her further down. Struggling, this time for air, Dianne wriggled out, and put her feet down in an effort to find the bottom, though the swift flowing current made it difficult.

To her surprise, she found that her feet could touch the bottom, and she burst forth into the air, gasping for breath. The water reached just to her chest, but it was a strong flowing current, and Dianne still struggled to prevent herself from being washed away.

Richard had quickly righted himself, and found it easier to stand against the water. He automatically reached his arm around Dianne's waist, and dragged her through the water to a place further downstream where the bank eased smoothly from the water course.

It was only a matter of minutes before he had deposited her safely on the muddy bank. Dianne's heart took a few minutes to slow down from racing as a result of the shock and effort. When it did, and she had taken stock of the situation - her aching muscles, cold wet clothes clinging to her skin, and her face and hands splattered with mud - she began to feel deeply upset. It wasn't the discomfort that caused her distress more than the fact that she felt irresponsible and foolish, and that it had to be the schoolmaster who had to rescue her from the whole disgraceful fiasco. What made matters even worse was that she had not only found herself in a dreadful predicament, but had literally pulled the dignified, serious Richard in with her.

She kept her gaze down, afraid to meet the familiar disapproving glare. She was certain that by now he must be blazing with fury. It was all she could do to prevent herself from dissolving into tears.

The memory of her terrified class finally prompted Dianne to pull herself together, and she made a move to get up, resolving to face the angry rebuke of the schoolmaster later. As she began to get up from the ground she felt a hand on her shoulder.

"Are you all right?"

Surprised, Dianne lifted her eyes to meet Richard's gaze, and was astounded to see genuine concern in his expression.

"Why...ah..yes!" She stumbled over her words, shocked at the unexpected thoughtfulness. "Uh...I'm sorry, Mr. Schrouder. I should have....I mean....I didn't know..."

"It's all right, Mrs. Pierceson," he spoke calmly, "but let me just say, I hope you don't make a practice of coming to school looking like this!"

Dianne threw her attention to her dishevelled appearance, and coloured at the mention of it. "I don't know what to say..." she stuttered.

"Well, I must confess, I have seen you looking better!"

Dianne had just taken offence and was feeling all indignant, when she was arrested by the sound of a deep resounding laugh. She stopped her prepared retort instantly and was astonished to see for the first time in their acquaintance, Richard's face alight with what looked like laughter.

She stood in stunned silence for a brief moment. This was the very first time she had ever seen an expression on his face other than severity. It seemed quite out of character, and she didn't quite know how to take it.

Later, as she changed out of her drenched clothing in the safety of the Todds' spare room, Dianne began to ponder the whole experience. Apart from the shock of having fallen into a flooded creek, Dianne was still trying to come to grips with Richard's laughing at her. He hadn't meant to be mocking or derisive. He had been genuinely amused. And she couldn't get over the fact that the laughter changed his face completely. He seemed to regain his youth almost instantly.

He should laugh more often, she thought to herself. *It is a vast improvement.*

Dianne's thoughts were interrupted by Mary-Ann, as she entered with a towel and bowl of warm water.

"Thank goodness he was decent enough to pull you out," she said loudly. "I shouldn't have wondered if he'd have let you be washed clean away!"

Dianne didn't answer the landlady's outspoken opinions, but in her heart she knew that Mary-Ann Todd held some ideas about Richard Schrouder that simply weren't true.

Chapter Ten

The weeks following the creek fiasco moved by quickly. Dianne had returned to her classroom dry, but somewhat shaken by the mishap. To her great relief, Richard said nothing more on the subject, in either rebuke or jest.

Richard Schrouder, who had briefly emerged from his hard protective shell to reveal a humorous nature, retreated immediately back into himself. It frustrated Dianne to some extent. There were moments when she could almost believe that Richard was a normal human being, but on the whole, the way he presented himself to the public in general seemed only to confirm what all the busy tongues of the town were saying. Dianne wanted to see beyond the indifferent façade, to see if there was a spark of human relationship which might be encouraged, but his response did not show any.

All in all, Dianne had to set him aside as someone worth knowing beyond their professional relationship. There was too much about him that was a mystery, and there was no openness from his side.

As each week passed the insecurity about her teaching position began to fade and she flourished in the classroom. The children responded with great enthusiasm and affection making her forget all Richard's early warnings about not becoming too attached to them. But he had warned her, and she had been lulled into a false sense of security which had to eventually reveal itself. That revelation came one fine spring afternoon.

Over the period of time she had been at the Carlton School, Richard had regularly given her the responsibility to oversee both classes for the afternoon. In her first few weeks she had wondered what was so important for him to do that he would leave her to take on his teaching responsibilities as well as her own. But she quickly suppressed that question, and instead took encouragement from the fact that he apparently needed and trusted her at least that much.

One particular afternoon, Dianne was conducting the usual religious instruction period. She had sat the children down, introduced the subject of forgiveness to them in great depth and detail, and was ready to read the prescribed portions of Scripture, only to find that the school Bible was not in its usual place.

When she asked the older students if any of them knew where Mr Schrouder might have put it, she got several suggestions but all of them proved fruitless. She turned back to the bookshelf where it should have been and made another thorough search. But the Bible simply wasn't there.

It was annoying to have the whole lesson interrupted by not having the required text available. She had put a lot of thought into the lesson, and was not prepared to do any other subject, so she asked Ted Jansen if he would go next door to the schoolmaster's residence to ask him where he had placed the Bible. She was surprised when Ted hesitated. At first she was tempted to scold the child, but took another tack.

"Ted!" she spoke in a firm but calm tone. "I don't expect you to refuse to obey my direction!"

"I'm sorry, Mrs. Pierceson!" Ted sounded truly regretful. "Mr. Schrouder has told us we're never to go to his house for any reason."

Dianne had been aware that the children gave a wide berth to the gate connecting the two properties, but suddenly she put it all in the context of what he was hiding in his home – or whom.

"Thank you, Ted," she dismissed him quickly. "If you children will sit quietly for a few moments, I will run next door and ask Mr Schrouder myself!"

Dianne slipped out of the front entrance, down the steps, and began to make her way toward the gate that joined the two properties. The closer she got to the house, the more her imagination sparked into life. Suddenly Ted's apprehension began to weigh on her mind and she wondered if Richard Schrouder was really hiding something dark and sinister.

Mary-Ann Todd's voice began to echo in her mind, as she remembered the mysterious unknown wife and baby.

Some say he's gone and knocked her off!

The phrase burned in Dianne's memory. She had never been overly suspicious before, but all at once the many unanswered questions came rushing into her mind, stirring up an unreasoning anxiety.

Don't be ridiculous! she scolded herself. *I know he likes to keep his personal life private, and that's nothing to me. There's no need for all this shivering.*

She was quite annoyed with herself to find that she had begun to tremble; but in spite of her wild imagination fuelling this stupid fear, Dianne forced herself on toward the front entrance of the Schrouder home.

She waited a minute after having rapped sharply with the front-door knocker, but it became apparent that no-one was going to respond. She heaved a sigh of relief, and turned quickly back toward the gate. One part of her, the silly, easily frightened part, wanted to rush back to the relative security of the classroom full of children, but even as she started in that direction, another part of her pulled her up.

I've got to have that Bible for the lesson, she thought to herself. *I haven't anything else prepared, and I can't just sit them there for the whole afternoon, just because some silly rumour has given me the heebie-jeebies!*

Determined not to allow her imagination to get the better of her, Dianne decided to check behind the house, wondering if perhaps the schoolmaster might have used his afternoon off to do gardening. She began to justify it to her scattered nerves by guessing that they were probably in the back yard working and hadn't heard her knock. But when she had looked thoroughly around the back garden and saw no signs of any person at all, her thoughts continued to tumble out of control.

As she approached the back door she had to talk really sternly to herself to pull herself together, to remain determined, since she needed the Bible, and if she gave in to her anxieties she would have to return to the classroom empty handed.

But despite her firm knocking, there was still no response.

They've gone out, she finally concluded, suddenly feeling a little foolish about her silly imaginings. *There's an afternoon wasted!*

But before Dianne turned from the door, something prompted her to try the door handle. It was a sudden impulse to try one last time to reassure herself that everything that could be done had been done and she was rewarded with the handle unlatching the door, and it gave way to the light pressure she applied to it.

A wave of guilt flowed over her as she peered inside the forbidden house. "Mr. Schrouder!" Her voice seemed to echo through the back porch, but still it brought no response.

This is ridiculous! she summarised her feelings. *They're obviously out!*

Just as she began to pull the door closed, she heard footsteps resounding on the wooden floor-boards of one of the inner rooms. A strong sense of curiosity urged Dianne forward, and she stepped fully inside the back porch.

"Mr. Schrouder!" She repeated her call, hoping that either he or his wife would quickly answer, but to her great puzzlement, nobody came.

I know somebody is there, she thought to herself, *and yet they are deliberately ignoring me. That would be just like him!*

An anger began to burn inside as Dianne considered what it was she needed and the apparent apathy of her employer. *I don't care if this is his private residence,* she fumed. *I have a class waiting on a lesson, and he only needs to give me a moment's attention.* Dianne began to reason away her guilt and apprehension. She continued further into the house toward the room from where she'd heard the movement.

She paused just before the door as she heard the movement again, behind the closed door.

"Mr. Schrouder!" She called again, a hint of impatience in her voice. Stepping forward, she knocked firmly on the wooden door. But again he didn't answer, and Dianne was filled with indignation. *He is so rude,* she thought to herself. *I've had enough, especially when he goes off and leaves me to teach his class.*

Angrily, she went to turn the handle of the door, but was horrified when she saw that the door was locked, with the key protruding from her side of the door. All at once, the images of a poor little Mrs. Schrouder flooded into her mind, as she imagined the persecuted, mistreated spouse locked away in this room.

Her first impulse was to flee the horrible discovery, to get as far away as fast as she could, before he came home and found her there. And she would have, had she not heard a thump followed by a cry of pain from behind the closed door. Compassion and pity filled Dianne's heart, and for a moment she battled with the temptation to unlock the door. Though she very much wanted to get out and away from this horrible house, something urged her to investigate further and before she had time to change her mind, she had unlocked the door, and pushed it open.

The sight that greeted her was shocking at the very least. A young girl of about ten or eleven stood looking at her, a terror plain in her eyes. Her hair was a mass of knots, and her clothes old and ragged. Dianne was overtaken by an avalanche of mixed emotions. Fear, outrage, compassion and panic all tumbled about in her mind. One part of her wanted to run away as fast as she could, another saw the dreadful state of this child and wanted to reach out to her, and yet another part wanted to grab a hold of the schoolmaster and beat some sense into his cold cruel head. But she didn't do any of these things. Instead she thought she'd better reassure a very frightened child.

"I'm sorry, dear," Dianne stammered. "I thought you might have hurt yourself, and I just..."

She didn't finish the sentence as the girl cried out again, turned from her, and ran to her bed, where she promptly bent down and crawled beneath it.

"Miss," Dianne called to her. "Miss, I'm sorry! I didn't mean to frighten you!"

Despite her apology, the child didn't respond, and Dianne could hear only the low moaning of the little girl as if she were trying to sing away some torment from her mind. Whoever she was, she had obviously been a prisoner of this room for a long time. Suddenly, Dianne realised that her silly fears now had a foundation, and it almost overwhelmed her. She had found him out. It was true what people had been saying. He *did* keep his family locked away.

A panic began to grip her as she considered what to do with her discovery. Suddenly, she wished that she had not forced her way into this horrible house, but the scene was now clearly etched in her mind and there was no erasing it.

Much too late, she decided it was time to flee the house but before she'd even gone one step, the sound behind her made her stomach twist with fear.

"What's the meaning of this, Mrs. Pierceson?"

She knew instantly that Richard Schrouder stood behind her, and that he had seen her closing the girl's bedroom door. She turned around and saw him standing with an arm load of firewood, staring at her, his eyes blazing with fury.

"I...I'm just..."

"You're just leaving!" His tone was harsh and angry. "You may pack your things and get out of this town, at once!"

His words cut into Dianne's heart like a knife. In one angry sentence, he was destroying her livelihood, her desires and the attachments she had made over the last few months. And she knew full well that it was all an attempt by him to try to protect himself from discovery.

She spun around on her heel to look him straight in the eye, a righteous indignation taking control of her emotions and bolstering her courage.

"Oh, no, Mr. Schrouder!" she hissed through clenched teeth. "I'll not be unfairly dismissed and run out of town. I haven't done anything wrong. It's you who will be packing your bags when the school board finds out that you have your family caged up like animals. I wonder that you dare show your face in public at all. What sort of man are you, anyway?"

In the flash of a moment Richard threw the wood down on the floor where he stood, reached out his hand and grabbed her roughly by the upper arm, forcing her toward the back door. She struggled against him and broke free, but his roughness had alarmed her greatly. Her eyes smarted with tears, not just from the forceful physical action but the whole gamut of fear, outrage and horror, and she was not even certain that he might not do something else more ghastly. But that didn't bear thinking about.

"Get out of my house," he spoke in a low growl, "and don't let me see your face again!"

Dianne pushed quickly past him, a sob escaping from her throat as she did so. Once she found herself in the open air the sobs came quickly and frequently. She ran blindly around to the gate, past the room where the children waited, into her own empty classroom. There she sat down, sobbing without reserve.

Chapter Eleven

P eter Todd sighed as he hung up his hat on the stand in the corner.

"Well, Peter!" Mary-Ann demanded. "Did you get the money or did he try to man-handle you as well?"

"You can stay on with us," Peter looked sympathetically to Dianne. "We'll be willing to put you up. It doesn't matter about the money!"

Dianne shook her head, blinking back the tears that refused to remain at bay. "It's no good, Mr. Todd," she sniffled as she spoke. "I have got to find regular employment! I can't rely on your kind hospitality forever. I must find a means of supporting myself!"

"Yes, but dear," Mary-Ann continued. "You've only just enough money to get you back to the city. There won't be anything left to rent you accommodation, or to buy food!"

"There isn't even money to pay your fare," Peter interrupted breathlessly, obviously finding it difficult to divulge the information.

"What!" His wife flared. "Do you mean to tell me that monster has not even the honesty to pay this poor girl her rightful wages? Why, this is outrageous!"

Dianne looked up in anxiety to Peter, and watched as he prepared his full explanation.

"Now, Mary-Ann," he soothed. "It's not so bad as that!"

"Well, what is his excuse, Peter? I would like to know!"

Peter ignored his wife's outrage, and gazed directly at Dianne, speaking in a gentle tone. "He wishes to finalise some details, Dianne. He asked if you would be so good as to meet him in the classroom this afternoon, and he will pay you your due then!"

"As if she would go!" Mary-Ann fumed. "He knows full well that the girl is traumatised by what she's found out. She'd sooner die than see him again. It's another trick to get out of paying the money he rightfully owes her."

"Mary-Ann, please!" Peter rebuked. "I will go across with her. She won't have anything to fear!"

Dianne stood up at this point, and held up her hand to silence the argument. "Thank-you, Mr. Todd," she spoke quietly. "I will go alone. I need to apologise to him at any rate, and I might just as well get it off my chest sooner, as later."

Mary-Ann looked incredulous. "What are you thinking, Dianne? You can't go crawling back to him. There's no way he'll give you your job back, if that's what you're thinking. He's too proud and stubborn for that!"

"I appreciate your concern," Dianne rushed on, "but there are some times when a person needs to face the music for themselves."

"But what about the girl? What about what you saw?"

"I don't really know what I saw, Mrs Todd. I was too shocked at the time, and he didn't give me any explanation."

"No! Because he didn't mean for you to see it."

"No, he didn't!" Dianne said regretfully.

"But someone had to see it. What about the wife? Why has he got them locked up there anyway?"

"I don't know," Dianne answered soberly. "I don't know, but I do know that it isn't going to be any of my business to find out. I trespassed on his property and saw something horrible. I've told Peter about it, and I'm going to leave it up to him to deal with. As for me, I'm not afraid of him, that he will lock me up or anything. But I think if I'm going to leave here with a clean conscience, I'd better apologise for intruding into his private affairs in the first place. I just want to do that and never see him again."

Mary-Ann opened her mouth to protest again, but her husband held up his hand to silence her. "Let her go, Mary-Ann. She is right to want to set her side straight, at least!"

The morning passed by quickly, as Dianne packed her clothes into the large trunk, and she gathered bits and pieces from around the room. Lunch time passed and Dianne felt sick with anxiety, anticipating the final meeting.

Mary-Ann tried to discourage her one last time from going, before Dianne stepped outside and proceeded resolutely down the path toward the school.

The moment she set foot inside the classroom her heart began to hammer away with apprehension, as it had on that awful afternoon. She was taking deliberate deep breaths, determined to remain calm and unaffected before the man who had so completely intimidated her.

He looked up from his desk upon hearing her approach and their eyes locked for some moments. Dianne could not make out whether she saw anger, fear or regret in his eyes. He was so practised at masking his feelings, he gave nothing away. Eventually, Dianne took a deep breath and spoke boldly.

"Mr. Schrouder, I apologise for prying into your private affairs. I appreciate the opportunity of the few months of employment," she hurried on, not waiting for a reaction. "I have been very happy teaching here!" She swallowed the emotion that threatened to break her voice. "If I could trouble you for my past weeks' wages, I will leave and won't bother you any more!"

Richard continued to stare blankly at her for some moments, before he finally opened his mouth to speak. "Have you any employment to go to?"

The question was simple, but startled Dianne, who was not expecting any concern for her welfare.

"No!" she answered, a bit angrily. "You know that I haven't!"

"And money?" he pursued.

"I will have enough to take me from this town and out of your sight, if you will settle my wages."

"Mrs. Pierceson…" Richard began to speak, then he stopped and allowed his words to trail off, as if in thought. "I have not always been right in everything I have said and done, and have not always treated you fairly!"

Dianne clenched her teeth and kept her gaze on the schoolmaster, determined to feel no pity as he struggled for words.

"I mean to propose marriage to you!" He suddenly blurted the words out.

"Marriage!" She reacted immediately. "Marriage! Mr. Schrouder, you would be the last person in the world I would marry, even if you didn't already have a wife!"

Richard stood up, his own emotions suddenly flaring.

"My wife is dead, as is your husband, and let me make it quite clear from the start, that the proposal doesn't come from any personal affection!" He paused to glare furiously at her.

"What then, sir?" Dianne returned the challenge, hotly. "What other reason is there to engage in such a serious contract?"

He turned from her provoked. Dianne waited to see what he would do.

"Contrary to popular opinion, Mrs. Pierceson, I'm not totally heartless, and I will not be held responsible for turning a helpless woman out into the streets!" His voice was low and his words calculated. "You need support, and I need a housekeeper and nurse for my daughter. The proposal is a business arrangement, the marriage is simply to keep your reputation respectable."

He ceased his explanation, continuing to look at some spot on the wall away from the woman whom he had addressed.

"Why?" Dianne finally managed to loosen her leaden tongue. "Why can't you simply allow me to go on as I have been - keep me in my teaching position. I know the money was not very much, but it was enough!"

Suddenly, she realised tears were flowing down her face. "I don't want to be married again. I have my memories of Samuel! They are enough!" Somehow, Dianne didn't care whether the man before her condemned her for crying or not. She was past caring.

"What happened yesterday - you in my home," Richard fought to find the right words, "it was merely the excuse I needed to dismiss you. I would have had to do it anyway..."

"I can't understand you, Mr. Schrouder," Dianne burst out, confused. "You talk about responsibility. I have worked hard, and achieved good results. The children have responded well to me, and yet you have always been determined that I would fail, even before I started."

He swung around to face her, a fire lighting his dark brown eyes.

"It's true that I don't approve of career women, but I have seen your work, and have noted your success. The truth is, Mrs. Pierceson, that I would have had to dismiss you, no matter what your sex. Originally, I pleaded with the education department to allow me to put on a second teacher, hoping to upgrade our facilities and standards, and they agreed on the condition that I raised a certain amount to supplement your income. But the fact is that I have had no success whatever in raising that sum, and now I must face the fact that I have to run this institution alone. No replacement! Mrs. Pierceson, you have done well, but I can no longer afford to keep you!"

Dianne stared at him, stunned at his explanation, her mouth hanging open as she remained silent.

"But it is also the case," he went on, "that I cannot keep my house and nurse my daughter, as well as run the whole school!"

"Your daughter!" Dianne finally found sensible words. "Wouldn't she be better off out of her prison, and allowed to be educated with all the other children her age?" She knew her words were harsh, but once again, an anger and frustration drove her forward.

"I don't care to discuss the welfare of my daughter with you," he snapped. "I am offering you legitimate employment, with accommodation and food as payment. Do you want the position, or not, Mrs. Pierceson?" His features were hard set, and his tone clinical.

Suddenly, Dianne knew that she must at least consider the offer. It was true that to go now would leave her penniless and homeless, and lost in a city where there would be no care or concern for her well-being; but still there remained so many questions and mysteries about Richard Schrouder, not the least of which was why he kept his daughter as he did. With these thoughts constantly troubling her mind she didn't know whether she was willing to enter into the solemn and binding contract that he offered, even though it did present a solution to her most pressing problem of survival.

Eventually, the pressure of making a decision became too much for her. "I don't know!" she cried, genuinely troubled. "I don't know you! I don't understand you! I don't even know if I can trust you, and yet I can't see that I really have any other choice!"

Despite her resolve to remain calm, pent up feelings got the better of her, and her voice wavered and cracked. "If only Samuel had stayed home from that parish meeting, I would be home with him now, and wouldn't be here facing this awful decision!"

Richard watched her impassively, making no move to bring either comfort or condemnation.

Finally he broke the tension.

"I understand your misgivings," his tone was still even, "and if it is of any comfort to you, I can only offer you the promise of a divorce, once some more suitable arrangement can be made."

"I don't believe in divorce, Mr. Schrouder," Dianne returned.

"Neither do I, Mrs. Pierceson!"

Dianne left the meeting overwhelmed and totally confused. He had refused to talk about his daughter or his wife, and this still weighed heavily on her mind. She couldn't think of any reasonable explanation for the situation. And yet he had intimated that his daughter needed a nurse. Did that mean that there was something mentally wrong with her, or some serious physical problem? More questions and no answers. Dianne didn't go back to the Todds as she had to think this through for herself. She knew what they would say. There wouldn't be any question that she should refuse. That answer was already well and truly ready in her own mind. What she needed to think about was the other option, whether she should accept, what that would mean, and whether she could live with it.

It was nearly nightfall by the time she returned to the Todds and they were nearly frantic, expecting her back much earlier. But at least Dianne had made a decision. She asked the Todds if she might stay with them for another week while she finalised things with her teaching role. Of course they only insisted that she stay longer. For the moment, Dianne knew her course.

Chapter Twelve

D ianne stood next to Richard in the small church office. The situation bore no resemblance to the full traditional wedding that had been hers seven years previously, with church bells, and a beautiful white gown.

Now, she stood in her ordinary school clothes, twisting Samuel's wedding band nervously on her finger. The Reverend Andrews stood before them with his wife, and he spoke in a gentle tone.

"You understand the seriousness of the covenant you are about to enter?" He looked first to Richard, and then to Dianne, for confirmation.

"Look, Reverend," Richard broke in. "I don't mean to sound hard, but all we need is the legal document. Mrs. Pierceson has agreed to live with me as my housekeeper and nurse for my daughter, so it would do just as well to skip over the love and commitment part. Neither of us is here for that reason. I only wish to keep her reputation intact!"

Reverend Andrews sighed as he listened to the schoolmaster's explanation. "Are you sure, Richard?" he asked searchingly. "As I said to you last week, marriage is not something to be taken lightly!"

"Well, do you think it is better for her to move in with me as she is?" His tone was impatient.

The minister shook his head. "All right, son," he soothed. "If you would just repeat the vows of commitment and faithfulness, at least, and sign the documents, I will see that Mrs. Pierceson...excuse me, Mrs. Schrouder's reputation remains above reproach!"

Dianne felt numb as she absently repeated Reverend Andrews' words. They held no meaning or significance, as they had when she'd looked lovingly into Samuel Pierceson's eyes and repeated them. She heard Richard mumble over them as well, and knew that they held even less meaning for him.

They mechanically signed the marriage contract, which fulfilled the legal requirements. Mrs. Andrews stepped forward to kiss Dianne on the cheek.

"I pray for God's blessings for you both," she murmured softly.

"Yes, and I too," her husband added as he extended his hand to Richard in congratulations.

Richard took the minister's hand, and shook it unconvincingly. "Thank you, Reverend," he spoke hurriedly, "but I do hope you understand the conditions of this contract. It's not like other weddings, you know that." He continued to search the minister's face for a sign of comprehension.

"I know what you have in mind, Richard," he responded, "but I will continue to pray for God's blessing on your lives, none-the-less."

Dianne followed quietly as her new husband strode out of the church office, the folded marriage licence in his hand. She wondered what the townspeople must be thinking, seeing them walking silently down the main street, he walking briskly, apparently confident, and she trotting timidly behind, struggling to keep up with him. He stopped suddenly outside the residence gate and turned back toward her, waiting as she puffed her way to come alongside.

"Do you want me to help you bring your things across from the Todds'?" The question was simple, but lacked any real concern.

"No! Thank you, Mr. Schrouder. I will ask Mr. Todd to help me with them!"

"As you wish!" He turned instantly toward the house and continued on up the path.

Dianne wanted desperately to sit down and cry, but she knew that she must now confront the barrage of negative comments that would be fired at her from the Todds. She had not told them of her decision, letting them believe that she would eventually return to the city. That was what they had assumed, and she hadn't corrected them. So now she would tell them of her choice.

"My dear child!" Mary-Ann's reaction was instant. "Whatever are you saying?"

The long-suppressed tears finally gave way, and burst forth in a torrent. Mary-Ann bustled directly over to her, arms outstretched and crooning her sympathy. "There, there, dear!" she murmured. "We can soon set it to right. Such contracts are easily broken if seen to straight away!"

Dianne pulled her head back from the landlady's shoulder, and shook her head in resignation. "No, Mrs. Todd!" She swallowed and pulled herself together. "I have made my decision! This is the only course of action available to me, and I have no choice but to follow it!"

"There must be other ways, Dianne," Peter ventured his opinion at last. "You don't have to go through with this marriage. Neither of you are happy about it!"

"Neither of us is totally happy either way, Mr. Todd," Dianne said rather defensively. "I have already accepted

Samuel's death, and it wouldn't matter whom I'm with. No-one can replace him!"

"But, Dianne," Mary-Ann continued to object. "He is so....so..."

"Whatever, or whoever he is, Mrs. Todd," Dianne cut in, "I have promised to serve him, and his poor, little daughter. In exchange, I will be provided for. It is a legitimate set-up. I know that it isn't the happiest of unions, but at least we can meet each other's needs!"

"All right, love," Peter sounded as if he accepted the explanation, though reluctantly. "I'll help you across with your things, but I want you to remember that whenever you need us, no matter what for, we will welcome you here with open arms. Will you promise to take me up on that?"

Dianne nodded meekly, a deep appreciation of them rising up within her.

"Thank you, Mr. Todd, Mrs. Todd," she whispered. "Thank you for all that you've done for me. I will always be indebted to you!"

"Nonsense, child," Mary-Ann protested. "It's no more than I would have done for anybody. And I will expect you to pop across to see me often. Do you hear me? Don't you go locking yourself away like...." She thought better of mentioning the former Mrs. Schrouder, and instead gave Dianne a firm hug. "Don't become a stranger to us, Dianne!"

Dianne stood silently in the back porch surrounded by her luggage, and waited as Peter Todd said goodbye and finally left her alone with her husband. The stony silence lasted some minutes longer, but Dianne had no courage or motivation to speak.

"There's an old mattress out in the shed," Richard eventually spoke. "I'll put it in my office for you. It's the room opposite the lounge if you want to start taking your things in."

He disappeared through the back door and Dianne let a sigh of relief escape from her lips. At the time she had signed the marriage contract, she had not known whether he expected her to share his bed as well as his home, but now it became apparent that she was at least to be granted her privacy at night, and for this she was very grateful.

She had moved all but the large heavy trunk by the time he returned inside with the mattress. "The linen press is in the hall," he informed her as he struggled past with the large cumbersome matress.

"Mr Schrouder," she called after him as he continued toward the office, "about your daughter."

He continued to position the mattress on the office floor as if he had not heard her.

"Please, sir," she persisted, "Must she remain locked up in her room? I mean, that is not really the most humane thing for a man to do to his own flesh and blood."

He swung around angrily, causing Dianne to step back in alarm.

"Mrs Pierceson," he hissed. "Since you are now her stepmother, I am obligated to inform you about her, but I most certainly resent your inferences."

"Mr Schrouder," she said furiously, "firstly, I am no longer Mrs Pierceson, in case you had forgotten, and secondly, if you do not make your intentions clear to me, what other conclusion am I to draw?"

He huffed loudly, obviously annoyed at having to tell her what she was insisting upon knowing.

"Since I can no longer call you Mrs Pierceson, and I will not call you…" he paused, obviously troubled by past memories. "I trust you will not be offended if I call you Dianne."

"It seems sensible sir, for a husband to call his wife by her first name, and I trust you will see the equal logic in my calling you Richard."

He ignored the comment and went on. "My daughter, Dianne, is totally deaf, and has been from birth. There is no way to communicate with her and she is kept in her room as a precaution for her own safety, especially since I have been away from her so often to do my work."

"Deaf!" Dianne whispered the word, shocked at this revelation.

"I expect you to see that she gets food, and if you could get her to wash occasionally, but above that, there is nothing else to be done for her." His voice sounded cold and unfeeling.

"But what of...I mean, can't you..." Dianne fumbled for words.

"Whatever else you do with her is your choice," Richard continued. "However, I forbid you to make her the laughing stock of Carlton. The town gossips know nothing of her, and I want it kept that way. Do I make myself clear?"

Dianne swallowed the large lump in her throat. She'd not had any idea that the schoolmaster had been struggling to maintain a handicapped child without any assistance whatsoever. Suddenly, things that had seemed so sinister last week took on a whole different light. Oh, she still couldn't understand why he seemed hard-hearted, but there had been something wrong with the child, and she could now see why she had been locked in the room. It made her terribly sad.

"I also expect you to see to all the household tasks: cleaning, cooking, mending and washing. For this service, I

will allow you to remain under my roof, and will see that
there is sufficient food for you to prepare. If there is ever
any item of clothing you need, please let me know and I
will assess whether the buget will allow it. Other than that,
you are your own person. I expect nothing else."

Dianne continued to stare blankly, long after he'd left her
room. She had just heard her employment requirements just
as she had on her first day at teaching, but somehow she
couldn't place her role correctly. Her title was officially Mrs
Schrouder, and yet she felt no more than a common
domestic who had just been hired. Dianne began to pull
her emotions into line as she understood that there was no
relationship to be had. There was no more need to fear
Richard Schrouder than she had when she was in his
employ as the second teacher.

Chapter Thirteen

When it came time for the evening meal, Dianne prepared some chops she'd found in the kerosene refrigerator, and some vegetables, and put together a bread and butter pudding for dessert. She was aware that the child would also need to eat, but was now quite apprehensive about how she could manage this. She'd only seen her the once on that unfortunate afternoon of discovery, and all those feelings seemed to sap her confidence.

Just when she thought she would have to face this unknown situation alone, Richard offered to show her what to do. Dianne was very glad when he took up the keronsene lamp and led the way. She was still unused to having to carry her light with her, after living with the benefit of electric light for most of her life.

They entered the room together, and as on her first visit, Dianne saw the little girl race to her bed and dive beneath it looking out at the adults from underneath.

"Does she always do that?" Dianne asked.

"Mostly," Richard answered.

"Why?" Dianne asked further. "Is she afraid of you?"

"What are you trying to infer?" Richard reacted.

"I just don't understand why a child should hide away from her father?"

Richard was quiet for a while before speaking. "It would appear she is afraid of me," he admitted. "But I assume that is because she doesn't understand who I am?"

"Have you tried to make her understand?"

"Of course not!" he defended "She is deaf!"

"So you believe she is mentally deficient as well?"

"Yes!" Richard sounded annoyed. "I don't like the accusation in your tone, Dianne. Do you think I deliberately made her like this?"

Dianne stopped interrogating. She hadn't wanted to accuse him, but her curious nature was never satisfied with something if she thought there might be more.

"You just leave her meal on the table, and put the lamp high up on that shelf where she can't reach."

Dianne didn't mention the fact that the little girl could probably pull her chair over to the shelf if she had a mind to, but then Richard didn't believe she had the mental capacity to figure something like that out. Perhaps she didn't.

"Why haven't you brushed her hair?" Dianne eventually asked, her curiosity getting the better of her.

"I have the dickens of a time just getting her to wash!" he exclaimed. "I can't even imagine trying to take a brush to that hair!"

Dianne didn't say anything else, but followed Richard from the room, after leaving the food on the table. There were now hundreds of thoughts buzzing around in her mind. Ideas and questions. She determined that she would try some of the ideas. *That's what a mother would do*, she justified herself.

Dianne slept soundly amongst the cases and boxes that made up her belongings. She had retired early after having cleared away the evening meal. No further conversation had been exchanged during the meal and she had been eager to escape to the world of dreams, where her life was not so complicated.

The small office was overcrowded with the large roll-top desk and tall cupboard, making only just enough space for the single mattress and her collection of luggage. Dianne determined to set her room straight as soon as she had attended to the morning duties.

Just as at the Todds', there was no bathroom, and Dianne was forced to dress without washing first, having no idea where to find a wash basin or even a tap.

She found the small kitchen to be just as she had left it and went immediately to work preparing a breakfast for both her employer and his daughter. She was glad that at least some modern technology had reached the schoolmaster's residence with the presence of a kerosene refrigerator. Dianne was thankful that the food stuffs were at least easy and convenient to reach, and that she didn't have to be forever asking Richard for directions.

Richard appeared shortly afterwards, looking fresh and neatly attired, his face clean shaven and his hair neatly combed. Dianne mumbled a good morning, even though she felt quite awkward. She recognised that she could now consider this house as her home, but it didn't feel anything like a place where she could feel at ease. She felt very much like an intruder, and in her own heart, she knew that if there had been any other option at all, she wouldn't have been here.

"Mrs. Pierce....Dianne," Richard began, correcting himself as he spoke. "I see that you need a wash basin and mirror."

Dianne flushed as she realized that her appearance must have been frightful, and worse, that he had noticed.

"You can use my basin and mirror after breakfast, and I will see that you get one of your own before tomorrow."

Dianne felt thoroughly disgraced, and with her injured pride could only manage a nod.

Richard didn't linger long over breakfast, and was gone the moment he had finished. Once again, Dianne breathed a sigh of relief and felt a renewed courage to face the day's tasks now that she was left alone to straighten out her feelings, then the house.

Armed with new confidence, Dianne decided that Richard's daughter would be her first job for the day. She took the plate of breakfast in hand and approached the locked door.

With the benefit of daylight, Dianne was able to take a better look at the little girl's room. It was sparsely furnished with the bed and one cupboard, a commode and the small table and chair that stood in the middle of the room. Dianne closed the door behind her and crossed to the table, placing the plate down there. As on her previous visits the child had dived under her bed as soon as the door had opened.

"I don't even know your name." Dianne's voice echoed around the room. "Not that you could hear even if I spoke it. Whatever will I do?"

Dianne knew that if she left the room the child would come out from beneath the bed and devour the food, but somehow she felt as if it were barbaric to treat the child like an animal at the zoo. She hadn't quite formulated a plan yet, but she was sure that there must be something she could do to make these visits into something more civilised.

"Well, I'm not sure what to do, child," she spoke to her, a smile on her face. "But one thing I am sure of is that we cannot let you go on living life like this. What do you think?" She forced what she hoped was a pleasant smile in the child's direction, but only received a blank stare in return.

"This is quite ridiculous, isn't it?" Dianne asked, knowing that nobody heard her. "Perhaps I shall go mad!"

She laughed at her own joke. She had no intention of going mad; only of finding a way to improve this situation. It was something she was going to think about until she found some strategy to succeed. That Richard might scoff at her thoughts was not a consideration. This was not something she was going to discuss with him. Just so long as she didn't parade the child around Carlton, and make her a laughing stock. She had no intention of doing that.

Dianne went back to the kitchen to wash up the breakfast dishes. Though she had heard what Richard had said about using his bowl and mirror, she felt totally intimidated by the prospect of trespassing on what she considered almost sacred territory, but her need was evident, even to herself though she couldn't see her reflection. She felt unwashed and undone, and so she talked herself out of her trepidation and walked into the master bedroom.

The room was not untidy, even considering a male occupant. There were little things about its decoration that hinted that there had been a female resident at one time. The curtains were a delicate lace, certainly not masculine in taste or style, and the bedstead was one that Dianne imagined could only have been chosen by a woman.

"Poor Mrs. Schrouder," Dianne whispered. "I wonder what became of her!"

That thought led her to thinking about the townspeople and their perception of their schoolmaster. In one thing they had been right. He had his family locked up – well, his daughter at least. But they had no idea of the reasons behind it. Dianne wondered if she should tell the Todds all about it, but hesitated. Why had Richard not told them? Why hadn't he told anybody? Why was he so cut off from everybody; that he didn't feel he could trust anyone with this information?

Dianne decided to wait and see what unfolded. She was not afraid of her new husband. She knew he was closed and wanted everyone to believe he was stern, but she didn't believe for one moment that he was the monster Mary-Ann Todd believed him to be. There was something else at the bottom of this complex family. Whether she would ever find out what it was or not remained to be seen.

Dianne had established a routine and was so efficient that she found she had hours on her hands when there was nothing to do. She carefully considered ideas of what she might do to change the little girl's situation. Many times she wished that she had someone to discuss her ideas with, but she didn't trust Richard's pessimistic attitude as anything other than a dampener on her enthusiasm, and the times that she did cross the road to take tea with Mrs Todd, she felt that it wouldn't be right to just blurt out the details; not without finding out first why Richard had not disclosed them before. Of course Mrs Todd had asked about the little girl, and Dianne had offered the excuse that the child was deaf and therefore handicapped. Mary-Ann had not wanted to let the schoolmaster off the hook. She fired other questions at Dianne, who didn't have any satisfactory answers. She knew that the situation was much more complex than simply a case of neglect on Richard's part, but there were so many variables that she didn't yet understand, so she always avoided the subject and tried to talk about things other than the schoolmaster and his daughter.

But that didn't stop her from thinking about the child, her situation and how it could possibly be changed. She thought about it a lot, and strategised. She'd asked Richard what her name was. At first he had been reluctant to tell her, maintaining that her name was of no consequence since she couldn't hear it. When Dianne pressed him further, he also restated his belief that the child was incapable of understanding and that Dianne shouldn't waste her time trying to communicate. Dianne had been cross with him and had told him so. She believed that even the simplest of souls could understand something, and she meant to try. As to a waste of time, she had plenty to waste!

And so armed with her name, Jillian, she decided to try an idea that had been brewing in her mind for a couple of days.

At the usual breakfast time, she bought in the tray of food, only this time she had two bowls of porridge and two spoons, and two glasses of milk. She set the tray down and immediately left the room and went straight back to the kitchen. Within a few moments she had returned bringing with her an extra chair. She placed it at the table, and sat down setting the bowls and spoons out neatly. She knew that Jillian was watching her every move, and so she sat down deliberately facing her, took up the bowl and began to eat. As she brought the spoon to her mouth she nodded to the staring child and smiled as she swallowed the cereal. Occasionally she beckoned to her and patted the other chair indicating the wish for her to join in the breakfast. But despite her best efforts the child did not move one inch from her haven.

Dianne was not too discouraged when she eventually took her plate from the room. She knew that the girl was not accustomed to any company, certainly not a relative stranger, and she did not expect any miraculous responses. However she deliberately left the second chair in the room and promised herself that, from now on, she would take her meals in the company of the silent child. While she justified this decision by saying it was for the benefit of the child, in the back of her mind, she had to acknowledge that it was also a good way to avoid sitting with the stern, often cross father.

Chapter Fourteen

Another argument had ensued when Dianne announced her intention of eating her meals in Jillian's bedroom. Richard couldn't see the sense in it, and Dianne couldn't understand why he couldn't see the good in it. Dianne had become convinced that if Jillian's mother had lived she would have pushed past this apparently impossible barrier. For some reason Richard couldn't see any hope, but Dianne was determined that in the absence of Jillian's mother, she would do her level best.

And so she established the routine of eating her meals in Jillian's bedroom. She doubted it would have made much difference to Richard one way or the other. Their mealtimes together had always been characterised by a strained silence. Short statements that communicated very little were about all that either of them had managed.

Once Dianne had made the meal times a familiar routine for Jillian, she decided to try something else. Richard had bought Dianne her own washbasin and mirror, and so she set them up in Jillian's bedroom, and every morning she attended to her basic wash and brushing her hair.

Jillian no longer ran to hide under her bed, but she still hung back from Dianne, shy and reticent. The young stepmother always beckoned to her, signalling and coaxing her to copy the daily routine. Several times Dianne had peeped through the keyhole and watched Jillian sit on the kitchen chair to eat her meal. Once she saw the child pick up the brush that she'd deliberately left behind. It thrilled her to know that the child was gradually gaining confidence. She was no longer as afraid of Dianne as she had been at first, and Dianne continued to talk aloud to her, no matter how ridiculous it seemed, and she used a lot of hand gestures and facial expressions.

One day a new idea came to her. She asked Richard if she could borrow some picture books from the school bookshelves, despite the fact that he had continued to deny the possibility of success.

"I don't know why you waste your time," he muttered. "She can no more communicate than fly to the moon."

Dianne had not bothered answering him back She had begun to feel that half of what Richard said to her was nothing more than a front to hide his deeper fear. She wondered if he made these loud protests more because he was afraid of failure, or worse, of success and all the implications that success would bring.

But success smiled on Dianne's efforts, though she didn't share all of the small signs of improvement with Richard. She didn't have confidence that he would understand, or even be glad about it, so she kept her successes to herself.

Several weeks later, Richard came in through the back door only a short while after he'd left to teach school. Dianne was startled as she had become used to the quietness that descended on the place once he'd left for the day.

"There's a parcel here for you!" He said, as if it were perfectly normal for him. "At least I imagine it's for you, since you're the only Mrs. Schrouder living, but I don't know who could be sending anything to *you*."

"Thank you, Richard," Dianne answered quickly, wiping her soapy hands on her apron.

She knew that the parcel would contain a book she had written away for. In her desire to help Jillian, Dianne had come to the conclusion that she needed some experienced advice, and had communicated with the city university, asking for a book on how to teach the deaf.

Rather than going straight back to his classroom, Richard waited and watched as Dianne eagerly opened the package. He noted instantly the gasp of joy as she saw the title on the cover: 'TEACHING SIGN TO THE DEAF'. The look of satisfaction on her face was such that Richard could no longer contain his curiosity.

"Is it your birthday, Dianne?" he asked, almost innocently.

She stopped studying the book and looked up at him, only just aware that he had remained behind and had been watching her every move.

"Oh! I'm sorry Richard," she looked confused. "Did you want something?"

He wished he hadn't asked, feeling that he had intruded too far into her personal space and had lost confidence.

"It doesn't matter," he said shaking his head. "I'd best get back to class."

Dianne allowed him to leave without trying to continue the conversation, but she had seen something and drawn a new conclusion – that he was on the outside, looking in. *He wants to relate, but doesn't know how,* she thought sadly.

But these melancholy thoughts didn't trouble her for long as she remembered the precious book that she at last had in her hands, and was ready to use. It was all Dianne could do to contain her enthusiasm while she finished attending to the household chores. She was very eager to get into Jillian's room and begin following some of the basic instructions outlined in the first chapter of the book. She began to entertain high hopes of success as she ran through each of the simple processes outlined, in her mind.

"Jillian!" She called out loud to the girl. "I have marvellous news. Just look what I have, Jillian!" she pointed excitedly at the new, hard-covered volume.

Jillian stood and looked at Dianne who had by now become less intimidating to her.

"Come on, little Jill," Dianne beckoned. "I've got a new helper, and soon you and I will be able to communicate."

Dianne sat down on her chair and patted the other chair for Jillian to join her.

"Dear Lord," she prayed aloud, "Help me to break through the barrier of silence, and help me to show love to this little child."

Dianne had prayed regularly for her new charge but never out loud while in her presence. Jillian moved over to the chair next to Dianne and amazed her teacher by sitting down.

"Oh sweetheart," Dianne exclaimed, overjoyed that the child had taken the first step towards her, "We are going to make it, aren't we!"

She reached out to touch her but Jillian pulled away quickly, frightened by the sudden motion.

"I'm sorry, little Jill." Dianne subdued her enthusiasm and composed herself. "I will have to slow down. Just a little bit at a time!"

Jillian gradually resumed her former position on the chair and watched closely as Dianne began to read. Following one of the simple instructions, Dianne took a pencil and paper and wrote down the word *book* in big bold letters. She held it up to show the silent observer.

"Book," Dianne overemphasised the word as she spoke.

"Book," she said again, as she picked up the instruction manual and held it out to her.

"Book," she repeated again as she indicated with her hands the sign for a book. She continued to repeat the process, emphasising the written word, trying to associate it with the actual object and the sign.

Jillian sat and stared blankly at Dianne, concentrating intensely yet without any apparent comprehension of what Dianne was trying to convey.

After some time at this exercise Dianne was frustrated but not defeated. She decided to try with a different object. There was a spoon left on the table after breakfast and Dianne chose this for her next trial. She wrote down the word in the same large hand, and continued through the procedure of holding out the instrument and making the appropriate sign.

A light of recognition crossed Jillian's face soon after Dianne had gone through the routine with the spoon. She reached for the silver piece of cutlery and held it in her own small hand for a moment. Then she looked up to Dianne and used the hand sign.

Excited, Dianne's face broke into a wide grin and she nodded her head vigorously. "Yes! Jillian, Yes! That's a spoon."

She hurriedly turned and picked up the book and handed it to the little deaf girl, then waited to see if she had understood. Within seconds Jillian began to use the appropriate sign for "book".

Dianne jumped up from her chair and clapped her hands, expressing her exuberance as if she were the child. Then, to her surprise, Jillian also jumped up and clapped her hands, with a tiny tentative smile.

"You've got it Jillian, I knew you could do it!" Dianne found emotion swelling her throat.

The day had simply flown by while Dianne had been working with Jillian. The pair had been actively studying and learning signs for hours without a break. Jillian's hunger to communicate seemed to be as intense as her teacher's and they had gone through as many objects as Dianne could find, writing the words, handling the objects and rehearsing signs.

"Oh my goodness," Dianne exclaimed as she noticed the sun dipping low in the sky. "Your father will be home at any minute, Jillian, and I haven't even given a thought to preparing tea."

Reluctantly she closed the book and gathered up her things, chattering as she did so. The look in Jillian's eyes was one of confusion and disappointment, and Dianne felt sorry that she was rushing out of the room without explanation. But there was simply no way as yet to explain, and so Dianne waved goodbye as she had always done and hurriedly locked the door behind her.

She had only just begun to peel the vegetables when Richard opened the backdoor and walked in. On every other evening, Dianne had the evening meal cooked and ready to serve by the time the head of the house walked in the door. Richard had never said anything about it either by way of gratitude or disapproval. But now, Dianne felt overcome with panic at having been caught far behind the schedule she had established. Her fingers seemed all thumbs as she imagined his glare upon her, making the already unfinished task harder to complete. Finally her anxiety became too much for her, and she dropped the peeling knife in frustration.

"I'm sorry Richard!" She spun around to face him. "I didn't mean to forget the time, but I just got so caught up..."

She stopped in the middle of her excuse as she saw there was absolutely no change in his expression, one way or the other. Sighing deeply, she turned back to the task but she was inwardly upset. *He's so intimidating,* she thought. *I always feel so inadquate, as if there's always something wrong. I wish he could be happy, just once.*

Richard retreated quietly to the lounge while Dianne continued to prepare and cook the meal. Once everything was on the wood stove, she decided to take her courage in hand and face Richard once again.

"I don't expect you to understand," she began, "but I have spent the entire afternoon with your daughter, teaching her signs. She has been almost as excited about it as I was, and we've achieved an amazing amount in this one afternoon." She spoke not really expecting much in the way of response. She watched and waited for the usual period of silence, but was very surprised when Richard actually spoke in a quiet, almost hopeful tone.

"Do you think that she actually understands you?" There was a definite note of uncertainty in his tone.

"Of course she does, Richard," she answered quickly. "She's only deaf. There's nothing wrong with her intelligence."

"I find that hard to believe!" There was just a hint of his former scepticism still in his voice.

"Then come and see for yourself," Dianne challenged him. "To watch her today, I'm telling you she wants to learn and she wants to communicate. I believe you have a very intelligent child there."

Even as she turned and walked toward the locked room, she knew that if she were right about Jillian's intelligence, that would make a huge load of guilt for Richard to acknowledge. After all, he had kept her for years under the misconception that she was incapable of learning. But Dianne was not going to keep up that façade just to pander to his feelings.

"Jillian," she called, then paused as she realised she'd yet again forgotten to get a lamp. But before she could turn to get one, Richard had brought one over with him and handed it to her.

"Thank you," Dianne said quietly.

Jillian looked up eagerly when she saw Dianne enter, and began to walk towards her, but when she saw her father behind she stopped and instantly ran for the cover of her bed. "Jillian," Dianne cried, distressed. "Don't hide, sweetheart. It's your father. There's nothing to be afraid of."

"I told you, didn't I?" Richard sounded relieved, though he used a resigned tone. "She can never be anything more than she already is."

Dianne swung around to face him, suddenly angry at his willingness to accept defeat. "Just stop it," she said firmly. "I'm tired of your...your scepticism. Jillian is intelligent. She learned so much this afternoon. If only you would stop your defeatist attitude and reach out to her – show her that you care ... "

"This is just nonsense," Richard argued. "How can I possibly show her anything at all, let alone that I care?"

"Why is she so afraid of you Richard? That is the question."

"She always hides under the bed when I come in. Always has!" Richard sounded defensive.

"But what have you done to make her so afraid?"

"I haven't done anything!" he said indignantly.

"You've never touched the child?"

"Of course. I've had to make her wash sometimes. Even you would agree to that."

"But wash times were a fight?" Dianne pursued, beginning to see what had been the past pattern.

"Haven't they been for you?"

Dianne didn't have the heart to tell him that Jillian had begun to use the basin and wash cloth herself, mimicking what she had observed in Dianne's own routine.

"And you've tried to brush her hair?" she asked.

"I gave that up some time ago," Richard said, still tense. "The screaming and kicking that went along with it just weren't worth it."

"Yes. I've not had much success there either," Dianne admitted. "Well, the damage has been done, so we must do what we can to make the best of it!" Dianne found she was suddenly full of nervous courage.

"What do you mean?" Richard sounded very unsure.

"I mean we must teach the child that you don't mean her any harm!"

"This is just a waste of..."

"And if you would stop looking so aggressive toward me," she pressed, cutting him off from an obvious attempt to retreat, "maybe she would feel a bit more secure, as if you weren't here to harm her."

"I've told you, I've never done anything to harm her, Dianne," Richard reacted back. "What do you think I am?"

"I think you are a man who has no idea how you present to others. Perhaps you don't know it, but you are positively intimidating. If I were to judge by the way you look I would be positively terrorised!" Dianne didn't know where the audacity had come from, but it was out, and Richard looked as if he had been slapped in the face. There was a tense silence for a few moments. With Richard looking stunned, and Dianne's shoulders all bunched up as if ready to launch out at him again, Jillian peered out at the feuding adults from beneath the bed, confused because she had never seen adult interaction before, and certainly not aggressive interaction.

"It can't be done, Dianne!" Richard finally broke the silence, doubt still very evident in his tone. "It's impossible!"

"Put your arms around me, Richard." An unexpected boldness possessed Dianne as a thought came to her mind.

"I beg your pardon?" He looked aghast at the suggestion.

"Just that, Richard," Dianne prompted. "Jillian has learnt what she has by example, so if you pretend that you love me and don't mean to hurt me, maybe she will learn to trust you."

"You're being ridiculous," he stammered.

"Just do it, Richard." Dianne was determined and she moved close to him and put her arms around his waist. She had never touched him like this before, but she was not going to think about the implications of it now. She had an idea and was running with it. At first she thought he would pull away, but eventually he put his arm around her shoulder, showing a reluctant willingness to try her plan.

Dianne smiled at Jillian as she stroked Richard's arm.

"This is your father, Jillian." She spoke the words confidently, while continuing to smile at the child. "See, love." She put her head against her stunned husband's chest and snuggled into his hesitant embrace.

"Please, Richard," she murmured quietly. "Just pretend. The only way to communicate with her is by example."

Eventually Dianne relaxed as she felt him reach his hand up to stroke her hair, and his other arm tightened slightly around her.

"Good," Dianne encouraged. "Now you're acting believable." Almost at the same time she pulled away and walked over to the table, taking up her pencil. She wrote down the word 'father' and took it over to the bed for Jillian to see.

"Father." Dianne spoke the word as she performed the sign.

"Richard, come here and let her touch you." Dianne had forgotten all about the tension that had existed between them moments before, and was intent upon the teaching routine she had established earlier in the day. She continued to point at the word and rehearse the sign.

Richard moved hesitantly toward the bed. As he approached Jillian moved further under the bed, still obviously afraid. Not to be outdone, Dianne got right down on her stomach to move close to the frightened child, and she reached out her hand. Jillian watched her stepmother closely, but didn't pull away. The atmosphere was tense as Dianne beckoned for Jillian to come closer to her, and for one awful moment Dianne was afraid that she had failed the test. But gradually, Jillian reached out for the paper on which Dianne had written the word 'Father'.

"Yes, Jillian," Dianne nodded and smiled at her. "Father!" Without fear of reaction, she shuffled out from under the bed, reached up for Richard's hand and, surprisingly, he allowed her to take it and draw him down to their level.

"Kneel down and let her touch you, Richard," Dianne coaxed, her attention firmly fixed on Jillian. She still held his hand, stroking it and trying to convey acceptance.

Richard was still apprehensive, but he bent down in response to Dianne's tugging on his hand.

"That's it," she encouraged, quite oblivious to his inner struggles, and only focussed on the lesson. "Here, Jillian. Father." She tugged at Richard's arm and pulled it out towards his daughter, letting go only a moment to perform the sign for father.

Jillian's eyes never left Dianne's face, looking for the reassuring smiles and nods of encouragement. Eventually the neglected little girl reached out and touched her father's hand.

"FATHER," Dianne signed as she spoke. "Father!"

Jillian smiled at her teacher and in turn, copied the sign.

Delighted, Dianne sat back and clapped her hands in triumph, laughing as she did so.

"You are so clever, little Jill. I knew you could do it!"

Richard, who had nervously and quietly submitted to the whole exercise, stood up, breathing deeply. There was a slump to his shoulders as he turned away from his wife and daughter.

At first Dianne didn't notice the strange despondency that had crept upon him, for she was still celebrating this most recent success. Jillian had also crawled out from beneath the bed and was clapping her hands to mimic her stepmother. Together, they were busily signing "FATHER", smiling as if they'd just won a prize.

"But I am just another object to her." Richard's voice was husky with emotion as he interrupted their display. "I'm just another toy in your game!"

Instantly, Dianne stopped and looked at him, understanding and empathy wringing her heart.

"At the moment, yes," she spoke carefully, "but you have never given her any example that you could be anything else."

"How can I, Dianne?" His voice was heavy with frustration and regret. "It's too late to be trying to make up for the past. I didn't know that she could understand. I thought she was just an animal."

"But she's not, Richard! She's not!" Dianne's voice was full of conviction. "Show her that you can love her. Show her!"

"I can't!" With this, Richard walked out of the room leaving Dianne to stare after him.

"What do you suppose the sign for stubborn is?" she asked Jillian, who only blinked at her in return.

Chapter Fifteen

Dianne's elation with her afternoon's success was deflated when Richard stalked out of the room, and to make matters worse, she found all the cooking dinner burned and stuck to the bottom of the saucepans. At first she was worried that Richard would be annoyed, but it seemed that he was too distracted to even notice that his dinner was ruined.

Dianne told him about the mishap, offering an apology and promised that she would soon fix something else for him to eat.

But Richard told her he wasn't hungry, and in those few words Dianne immediately sensed that something was wrong. His tone sounded utterly depressed. She knew the slump in spirits had nothing to do with the ruined dinner and everything to do with Jillian.

"I'm finding it difficult to understand you, Richard," she said straight out. "Don't you want to learn to communicate with your daughter?"

"It's not as easy as you make out, Dianne," he said.

"It will be a challenge to teach her how to communicate fully, I know that, but…"

"I'm not talking about teaching her!" Richard interrupted.

"Then what are you talking about?"

"You wouldn't understand."

Dianne was tempted to issue the challenge to him, to get him to try and make her understand, but she felt as if she had pushed him far enough in one evening. In fact, later, once she'd gone to bed and as she went over all the things she'd done and said, she began to feel absolutely horrified with herself. Her own reserve, born of being forced to marry a man she didn't know or love, seemed to have flown out the window, and as she lay, blinking in the darkness, she couldn't help but feel foolish for having been so bold and presumptuous.

The next day, Dianne got up determined to continue her work with Jillian, but resolved to be more circumspect when dealing with her husband. And so the lessons continued. Richard must have known what Dianne was doing, but he chose not to refer to it. Each night when she had served him his dinner, she left him and went in to spend time with Jillian. And on the weekends, when Richard could have spent more time at home, he chose instead to either work outside or in the school building, so Dianne's routine wasn't interrupted.

But the enthusiasm that came with every new lesson learned was becoming too much for her to keep to herself. She wanted to tell the Todds all about it, but still didn't feel that she had the right, so she decided to pursue Richard's approval.

"We have been making great progress, Jillian and I!" She made this announcement as she served dinner one evening, and it was really quite out of the blue. She hadn't made a practice of starting any conversation, and he was never the one to make any moves to talk, so her statement seemed to hang awkwardly in the air for a few moments. But Dianne didn't move off with her dinner to join Jillian. She stayed and looked at Richard in a manner that he couldn't avoid noticing.

"I assumed you would have," he eventually responded.

"Yes, she is a delightful little girl, and quite smart. It's a shame you don't try to spend some time with her yourself."

Richard had begun to eat, as if he was trying to ignore what Dianne was saying, and almost as if he hoped she would stop and go away. But she didn't go away, she stayed and continued to look at him in expectation of an answer. Eventually her silent stare won out.

"What is it you want me to do?" Richard burst out.

"Why don't you come in after your tea and spend some time with her. Let me show you how much she has learned."

Dianne could tell that he very much wanted to refuse, but her look was persistent, if nothing else, and he couldn't really find any reasonable excuse.

"All right!" he muttered. "Just let me finish my tea in peace, will you."

Dianne smiled, picked up her plate and went in to eat with Jillian.

Dianne had brought their plates out to the sink and still Richard hadn't gone to Jillian's room. She was itching to make some comment, but had made a strong effort not to be quite so audacious. She washed up all the dishes, dried and put them away before returning to Jillian's room. As she went to open the door, Richard approached her.

"So what is it you want me to do?" he asked, trying to mask his nervousness.

"I'm not sure," Dianne admitted. "Why don't you just come in for a while, and let's see what happens!"

Richard was not the enthusiastic optimist that Dianne was, but he quietly accepted her suggestion. Dianne wondered if there wasn't much more going on in his head than he ever let on.

Jillian's facial expression was easy to read when she saw her stepmother. She lit up with delight to see her, but instantly changed when she saw her father. However, this time, she didn't dash to her hiding place. She simply stood and watched him, then looked to Dianne.

"FATHER," Dianne signed for her, placing her hand on Richard's shoulder. "FATHER COME FOR YOU."

Dianne wasn't certain that Jillian was fully understanding signed sentences, but she had begun to use them in hopes that she would pick it up eventually.

"Smile at her, Richard," Dianne coached. "She isn't going to bite you." She thought it was a simple request, but when she looked up to see how he responded, she saw that he was really struggling.

"It feels so awkward," Richard said uneasily. "I have been in this room every day for years, and I have never tried to smile at her, or make eye contact."

That there were things that Dianne could have said in response to that tragic statement was irrelevant. Now was not the time to study past mistakes. Now was the time to take positive action.

"FATHER LOVE YOU," Dianne signed for Jillian, but Jillian's blank response indicated that she didn't understand.

"What are you saying to her?" Richard asked.

"I'm trying to communicate to her the concept of love. That you love her," Dianne answered.

"But how can you…"

"Let me try something," Dianne hurried on. She took her pencil and note book and wrote the word love. Then, after showing Jillian the note, she used the sign. But without a tangible object, Jillian remained confused. Dianne tried to reach out to hug her, but Jillian stepped back from her.

"All right then," Dianne said out loud, determined not to be beaten. "Let's try this instead!"

She held out the note and pointed to the word, used the sign, and this time approached Richard to hug him. "We're demonstrating the action," Dianne explained needlessly.

"Yes, I can see that!" Richard replied.

"But you feel awkward about it?"

"Well, I...yes."

"It just helps for her to see what I'm referring to. It would help if you played along."

Eventually he submitted to the embrace, and just as quickly, Dianne pulled away from it.

"FATHER LOVES MOTHER," she signed, then hugged Richard again. "FATHER LOVES YOU." This time she pointed to Richard and to Jillian, and held out her hand in hopes of coaxing them towards each other. Jillian looked carefully to Dianne for encouragement, and because of the trust that had been being established over the past weeks, she allowed Dianne to take her hand and bring her to her father.

"Gently now," she coached. "Just put your arm around her and give her a little hug."

But Jillian wouldn't let go of Dianne's hand, and pulled her into the hug as well. It was clumsy at best, but it was effective. Jillian stepped back and smiled at Dianne, clapping her hands in the way that had become familiar when they learned something new. Dianne smiled at her, but was aware that Richard was deeply affected by this simple action.

"I LOVE MOTHER; I LOVE FATHER," Jillian signed, proud of her new word.

"Do you understand what she's saying?" Dianne asked Richard.

When he didn't answer, Dianne turned to see why, and was shocked to see tears shining in his eyes. It was so uncharacteristic of the man she had known that it shook her.

Not wanting to draw attention to his display of emotion, Dianne simply smiled at him, hoping that he would be encouraged.

But he just followed his normal pattern and left the room without answering. It really bothered Dianne that he was so complex and hard to understand, but she couldn't follow him out. She needed to stay with Jillian and finish with her for the evening.

It was nearly an hour and a half later that Dianne extinguished the lamp, came out of the room and locked the door. She had developed enough trust with the child that Jillian now allowed her to tuck her up in her bed.

But it struck her that it was easier gaining the trust of the deaf child than that of her father. She considered quietly slipping off to bed and ignoring him, but some compassion remained in her heart, and she felt she could understand why he was finding this new relationship with his daughter so difficult. She decided to give him just the one opportunity to talk about it, but was determined to leave if he continued being defeatist.

"That was a very significant breakthrough with Jillian, don't you think?" she asked.

"I was happy enough before," he said cryptically.

"Happy!" Dianne cried. "What do you mean, 'happy'?"

"I mean I don't know that we should not have left well enough alone."

Dianne was dumb-founded. "You can't mean to tell me that you would prefer the lonely and isolated life you were living, no-one to love you, knowing that your little girl was right under your roof yet completely locked away from your affections?"

"You don't understand!" he burst out suddenly animated. "I've never loved anyone that it hasn't ended in being hurt. The more you love someone, the more it hurts when it all comes to the inevitable end!"

"Whatever do you mean?" Dianne was astounded by the strange explanation.

"I've learned by bitter experience that it's better to live as an island than give people the opportunity to turn on you later."

"Surely you don't think that of your own child?" Dianne couldn't hide her amazement.

"Of her, and of you! How can I allow myself to love either of you!"

"Well, firstly, I'm not asking you to love me," she was quick to re-establish that boundary. "We have our agreement and I'm happy with it. But as to your own daughter - Richard, you have got to love her. You can't deny your own flesh and blood!"

"I know that in my head!" he cried out, obviously distraught, "but you haven't had the benefit of cold hard experience!"

"Well, I don't know what experience you're talking about, but whatever it is, you'd be a fool to let it rule you your whole life!" She turned from him disgusted with his attitude. "One thing I do know is, I can't do everything for you!"

Dianne left and went to her bedroom feeling utterly deflated. She had recognised early on that Richard was going to find it difficult to break through with Jillian, but she had thought that he would be glad when he finally did.

Now that she had come face to face with his deep mistrust she didn't know what to do. She didn't really understand why he held such fears, and she had no idea of just how to help him to see past them. One bit of his conversation returned to bother her mind as she prepared for bed.

"As if I would want him to love me, anyway," she fumed. "It's bad enough that I have to be recognised as his wife without actually having to be affectionate with him as well. He is not the man that Samuel was!"

Dianne decided that it would be perfectly all right for her to tell the Todds all about the progress she had been making with Jillian. They seemed interested, and Peter particularly was very pleased to hear it. But Dianne asked them if they would not spread talk of Richard around the town. She felt rather sorry that he had been the subject of so much speculation, often false, and that so many people had passed judgement on him. Dianne knew that she had come to love Jillian very much, and she hated the idea of the townspeople talking about her in a careless fashion.

As the stepmother-stepdaughter relationship continued to grow, Dianne began to begrudge the time she was obliged to spend on the household chores, racing through them as quickly as possible in order to get back to Jillian's company and down to the tutoring.

After one particularly successful day, Dianne became possessed with the inspiration to bring Jillian out of her room. Making mental plans, she decided that it would be quite safe as she would keep Jillian with her at every moment, and she decided to lock the back door just as a precaution, though it did seem rather odd to think of the child racing suddenly for the back door, searching for a freedom she did not know existed. But Dianne was certain that Jillian could learn so many more things by being outside her room.

But her enthusiasm did not match the effort necessary to perform the task. Jillian was afraid and reluctant to venture outside the room that had been her whole world for almost eleven years. Dianne spent a lot of time coaxing and encouraging Jillian to follow her through the door, but Jillian remained rooted to the spot inside her room, some four feet away from the door.

Eventually, she gave up coaxing, knowing that her chores needed to be done, but she was not prepared to give up. She purposely flung the door wide open, and left it that way while she took up the task of dusting the hall table, directly outside.

Dianne waved and smiled at Jillian frequently as she over-cleaned the small area. But Jillian only stood and watched her teacher's every move, still unwilling to test the unknown. Finally, Dianne knew that she could no longer justify polishing the already gleaming hall stand, and so she moved on down the passage towards the kitchen, leaving the door still open.

Working away at the cleaning and dishes, she periodically poked her head back into the hall. It was on the fourth such check that she was delighted to see Jillian's own head looking in wonder at the world outside her room.

Dianne beamed at her and waved, catching her attention, and she continued to beckon her to come further. In response, the little girl smiled back, waving also, but still hesitating, still lacking the confidence. However, Dianne was encouraged and even more determined to succeed.

As she moved from room to room, cleaning and polishing, Dianne continued to refer back to the open bedroom door, and the little girl who peered out from it.

"Come on, little Jill," she finally became frustrated. "Come and help me." She held out a polishing rag to her, and signed for her to follow. Once again, she commenced rubbing down the hall stand, using it as an example, all the time turning to smile and hoping to build Jillian's confidence.

Gradually, Jillian moved out, looking about quickly as if afraid of the unknown world she had just entered, but Dianne continued to smile her encouragement and nod in affirmation.

"Good girl!" she cried. "You can learn to be my helper, can't you?"

Hesitantly, Jillian returned the smile, slowly brandishing her rag in keeping with Dianne's example.

"We're going to have one of the cleanest hall stands in the country, aren't we?" She spoke the joke aloud for her own benefit, while she beamed at Jillian.

By the time Richard walked through the door, at day's end, Dianne was humming with pride, having the dinner cooked to perfection, and, to his great surprise, the table set with three places.

"What's this?" he asked.

"I trust you will not object to your family joining you for dinner," Dianne answered smartly, waiting for his reaction.

"You won't get her out here, if that's what you mean." He sounded as if he were certain.

"She's already out! Has been all day, and is now waiting for "FATHER" to come home, so that she can surprise him." Dianne signed the paternal signal as she spoke.

Richard's expression didn't change from apprehension and uncertainty.

"Please, Richard," Dianne pleaded. "I can't do everything for you. You have to accept some responsibility to help yourself, you know!"

"I don't know that you might not be getting a little too outspoken, Dianne!" He seemed to be serious in his rebuke.

"I beg your pardon, Richard," she thrust back at him, sarcastically. "Shall I take our plates out of your royal sight? Would that please you?"

Her sarcasm cut deeply, and he instantly retreated into his shell. "Bring her in, if you will, then! But I don't think she is ready for it!"

Dianne swallowed the retort that occurred to her, and went to bring Jillian out to see her father.

"HAPPY FATHER?" the little girl signed as she entered the kitchen. For so long Richard had been hiding behind an indifferent façade that he nearly maintained his usual unresponsive expression, but he could not resist the plea in his daughter's eyes, and so he forced an uncharacteristic smile and nodded in acknowledgment, patting the chair next to him. To his amazement, she shook her head and crossed instead to Dianne, receiving from her the plate of food. With all confidence, she proceeded to place it on the table in front of her father.

"Thank you, Jillian," he responded verbally, automatically.

"You see!" Dianne jumped at the opportunity. "She is as normal as you and I!"

"Granted, Dianne," Richard conceded, provoked by her insistence. "Now, may I please have some peace and quiet while I eat my dinner."

Dianne beamed in triumph at Jillian, nodding her encouragement for the child, but more importantly, she inwardly acknowledged the victory of having won the schoolmaster's approval.

The dinner continued in silence, Jillian continually looking to both adults for their expressions of approval and encouragement. Dianne's heart was at bursting point, she was so happy to see the once-isolated child sitting in her own place at the family dinner table.

Dianne waited patiently for her husband to finish his meal before speaking again.

"Richard," she ventured cautiously.

"Yes!" His answer was gruff again, as if he'd felt too vulnerable with his sudden display of openness.

"I want your permission to have guests for dinner."

"Guests!" he cried. "What on earth would you want to have extra people here for, and who do you think would come in any case?"

"May I, please?" She injected all of her sympathy-winning tone into the request.

"Why?" He held out answering.

"Because I'd like to entertain my friends, and thank them for everything they've done for me. Is that so wrong?"

"What friends?" He fired another question at her.

"The Todds. They've always been so good to me, and I enjoy their company. Besides, it couldn't hurt you to have a little social interaction now and then!"

"I don't need any social interaction," he argued.

"But I do. Please, Richard. It means a lot to me."

"Look, Dianne," he glared at her, obviously struggling to maintain his usual grim expression. "Don't exercise your feminine wiles on me."

Dianne sighed as she admitted defeat. Jillian looked at her with concern in her eyes, having sensed that there was tension between the adults.

"LOVE," she signed to Dianne, pointing to Richard and then to her. Dianne laughed and was about to shake her head in denial to the girl's request, but when she considered the implications of such a refusal, she thought better of it.

"We'd better play the game, Richard," she spoke lowly. "Jillian doesn't want us to fight!"

"Don't use the child as an excuse to get your own way," he continued crossly.

"Richard," Dianne protested. "Look at her!"

Jillian stood, continuing to sign "LOVE," pointing at the two feuding adults.

"If we don't follow the sign, she will get confused!"

"How far can you go pretending to love someone?" Richard asked.

"Well, if we don't create the tension in the first place, she won't be asking us to resolve it, will she?"

Richard sighed, clearly still annoyed, and stood up to meet his determined wife in an embrace.

"You're not fooling her," Dianne warned him. "She can still see that you are upset with me."

"Next you'll be telling me that she wants to have guests to dinner as well! You two are both working against me!" He tightened his arms as he spoke, and finished the charade by placing a gentle kiss on her forehead. "Do you think she will believe that?" he asked as he turned back to his chair.

Dianne didn't answer, turning quietly back to the sink. She did not know what Jillian believed. All she knew was what she believed, and that was that her husband had meant the kiss to be affectionate. This realisation troubled Dianne deeply. Suddenly, having to consider that her relationship with Richard might be anything more than the business arrangement they had first agreed to, was very disconcerting. Dianne had always maintained that she would never marry again after Samuel, and when this marriage was her only option, she had decided that at least she would never love again. That was the foundation on which she had been living, and Richard's small revelation of developing affection made her uneasy.

Chapter Sixteen

R ichard reluctantly gave his wife permission to invite the Todds to dinner.

"I suppose there's no harm in asking," he conceded. "I doubt they'll come, anyway!" Dianne launched into a frenzy of cleaning and preparation. She held no doubt that they would accept her hospitable offer.

The actual invitation was a complicated process, as Dianne wanted very much for Jillian to see the "PEOPLE" before they intruded into her private world. She left Jillian at the front window, signing for her to watch while the request was made.

Dianne hurriedly entreated Mary-Ann and Peter to follow her down their front path to the gate, opening onto the road. The Todds were puzzled at first, until Dianne slowed down enough to explain the reason why she wanted them to communicate within sight of the front window.

Peter Todd responded warmly to Dianne's invitation, and expressed his anticipation of the event. Mary-Ann, however, remained reserved, but still managed to agree to come across as a guest to the schoolhouse. Dianne got both of them to smile and wave at the little girl, who peered out at them from behind lace curtains in the front window of the schoolmaster's residence.

"Every time we see her she seems to be more happy. I would never have expected it," Mary-Ann muttered to her husband, as they walked back to their little home.

"You forget, my dear, what Mr. Schrouder used to be like and how happy they used to be."

Mary-Ann gave a snort of disgust, unwilling to admit the truth, and bustled past her good-natured husband, determined not to concede any ground with regard to Richard Schrouder.

Dianne's excitement mounted as the time drew near for the planned evening. She found herself humming as she worked, and didn't even mind the negative comments that still came from her husband.

"I don't know why you want all of Carlton to be parading through my house," he said. "They are only a lot of gossips who've been waiting for the opportunity to find something else they can condemn me for!"

"Richard! It is not the entire population of Carlton, it's only the Todds, and they will not be able to find any fault with you at all, so long as you remember to smile occasionally and perhaps, if you could inquire about their health."

Dianne laughed under her breath as she lectured him. She had come to see glimpses of quite a soft-hearted character hiding behind his brusque manner. At times she had been astounded at the way he gave in to her whims. It was certain that he would nearly always object and protest, but he usually ended up quietly giving in, just when she least expected it.

Dianne realised that she could really take advantage of this characteristic in Richard, but determined not to. She could see that he was still suffering from something that had crushed him in the past, and while she didn't think she loved him, she really didn't want to add to his hurt.

Dianne coaxed extra hard for Jillian to allow her to brush her hair. It had been the one thing that she had been reluctant to force on the child, knowing that brushing normal healthy hair often hurt, and to try to pull a comb through this matted hair would hurt her a lot. But now Dianne really wanted to make a good impression on her very first guests since her time as Mrs. Schrouder.

"Honey, I know it hurts," she apologised as she tried desperately to get the knots out of the hair. "I'm sorry, but we need to do something with your hair sooner or later!"

Her verbal explanations had no effect on the deaf girl, who was already wincing as the brush pulled at the tangles. Dianne persevered for a while longer before she took pity on the child. She decided the only way to get that hair unknotted was to start again, and cut her hair short. But she felt she should have Richard's permission to do that, and so she went outside to find him, explain the situation and get his approval. Cutting her hair was not an easy task either, and once Jillian sat with her hair closely cropped to her head, Dianne breathed a sigh of relief. It didn't look very pretty, but at least she was now at a place where she could start afresh teaching Jillian to brush her hair and keep it clean and tidy.

"Well, at least you will look smart in the new dress that I've made for you," Dianne said, trying to find a positive aspect in the situation.

Since it was Saturday and therefore no school, Richard worked only half the day, and was in early. He usually spent most of his weekend either working at the school or tidying his own garden, cutting wood and other odd jobs.

When he came inside, Dianne found herself reminding him again about putting on a clean shirt, not forgetting to smile, and other things that she'd already said. And then she scolded herself again for nagging him.

The hours ticked by slowly, even though Dianne still had many things to prepare, but her excitement was such that she felt like a small child waiting for Santa to visit.

When she finally heard the rapping at the front door, she asked Richard if he would answer it. She noticed that he seemed reluctant as he dragged himself out of the lounge chair, apparently resigned to Dianne's plans. He was dressed in a clean shirt and had made sure his hair was neatly in place. She felt relieved that he appeared to be co-operating.

Dianne put the saucepan down when she heard Richard show the Todds into the lounge room, and hurried out to greet them. She was genuinely happy to see them and didn't hold back any affection in her greeting, hugging the older woman and receiving a kiss on the cheek from the husband.

"Thank you for having us, Richard," Peter looked to the reluctant host, who hung back from the exchange. "It was good of you to ask."

Richard nodded in acknowledgment, but Dianne could tell that he was uncomfortable.

"Come into the kitchen," Dianne directed. "There is someone I'd like you to meet."

The Todds must have sensed Richard's apprehension, and were glad to follow their hostess.

Jillian hung back in the corner at first, watching as Dianne seated her guests and poured them both a glass of lemon cordial. Then, after Dianne had briefly explained the procedure, she began the routine that had been the basis for all that Jillian had learned. She wrote down the word 'friend', made the sign and then shook first Mary-Ann's, then Peter's hand firmly. Jillian watched intently during the procedure, but was still reluctant to come forward.

"Perhaps if you sign for her to come," Dianne suggested.

"You realise that she's never met any strangers before, other than myself of course."

Mary-Ann took Dianne's advice immediately, giving the come signal, and smiling to her as she did so. Dianne moved to the corner and took Jillian's hand, as if to prompt her, and it seemed as if that extra effort inspired the confidence needed to bring Jillian out.

"FRIEND" Dianne signed, and shook their hands again.

"FRIEND" Jillian copied the sign and timidly took the two strangers by the hand, one at a time.

"She is delightful," Mary-Ann could not hold back her approval. "And such a pretty girl."

Dianne beamed proudly at the compliment, almost as if Jillian was her own child.

Jillian continued to impress the friends by assisting Dianne in serving the food. Peter and Mary-Ann chatted happily about the weather and other unrelated topics, but all of them were very much aware that Richard was struggling to interact. He was still in the other room, but nobody made any comment that would draw attention to his absence and therefore make the situation more awkward than it already was.

Eventually, the meal was served and Dianne signed Jillian to bring her father to the table to eat. Jillian instantly obeyed, and moments later brought Richard into the kitchen. Dianne thought he looked as if he'd have liked to just disappear, but Jillian holding his hand made it impossible.

"Could you say the grace, Richard," Dianne asked slyly, knowing that he would not refuse.

Richard spoke the mealtime prayer clearly and methodically, and no-one could have faulted its presentation. The meal was eaten in an atmosphere of friendly conversation, exchanged primarily between Dianne and her guests, much the same as it had always been when she was a guest in their household. Richard remained quiet as he ate, and yet, just according to Dianne's instruction, he did manage an occasional smile in response to some humorous remark or another.

Dianne signed for Jillian to help her clear the plates and was busy stacking the dirty dishes when she heard Peter Todd address Richard with a comment that made her immediately anxious.

"Your daughter is a delightful little girl, Richard," Peter spoke sincerely. "It must be a great comfort to you having her look so much like her mother!"

Dianne froze, waiting for a response from her husband, wondering what he would say at the reference to his first wife.

"I was very sorry to hear of her passing," Peter continued after some moments of strained silence. "I'm sorry we have left it so long in offering you our condolences."

Dianne couldn't contain her curiosity any longer. She turned slowly around to look into Richard's face, desperately hoping to see a positive response there, but to her dismay his face had hardened and it was painfully obvious that he did not mean to respond. Dianne struggled to find words that would break the tension, but before any sensible thought had been spoken Richard had stood up, without even an apology, and walked hastily from the room. It was apparent that he'd retired to the quietness of his own bedroom as they heard the door shut behind him.

Mary-Ann was bursting to make some appropriate remark concerning his lack of manners, but a stern look from her husband kept her silent.

"I'm sorry, Dianne," Peter gently ventured. "I knew it would upset him, but there are some things that he has obviously never faced – what happened to his wife is one of them!"

"I don't even know what happened to her," Dianne blurted out, the confusion evident in her voice.

"Nobody does, my dear," Peter continued calmly. "But what I do know is that Richard Schrouder has been struggling alone for too many years. I can see I should have been more forward when we realised something was wrong over here. Instead I didn't want to seem to be prying or presumptuous, and as a result one of our neighbours passed away, and nobody did anything about it. It is way past due, but time that somebody starts reaching out to Richard in genuine sympathy."

Dianne could not argue with Peter's logic, even though she could see that Mary-Ann was dying to.

"You understand I hardly know him, Mr. Todd," Dianne excused herself. "I am only really a housekeeper in this home. Nothing more."

"I know, Dianne," Peter reassured. "I'm not trying to make you feel as if it's your responsibility. I'm the one who has known him for years. I knew something was wrong years ago, but I didn't act. Now I regret leaving him his so-called privacy. I mean to start acting like the Christian neighbour I should have been."

Dianne was grateful for Peter's willingness to admit his fault and then take responsibility for it. She knew that what he'd said about Richard was right. Someone needed to be forward enough to show they cared, really cared, about the person of Richard Schrouder. Just to attend his house and child was not enough. He needed someone to help him face the past and the memories that still affected him. And

Dianne didn't have any confidence that she could be that person; but she did hold out hope that Peter would be the best person for the job.

The Todds stayed to eat dessert and Mary-Ann helped Dianne clear away the dishes. No more was said about Richard, and conversation turned to the light, unimportant things of everyday life, their best effort to pretend that the situation was normal.

But beneath the surface all three experienced mixed feelings. Peter was pondering his regret at having held back so long. His wife was frustrated, fuming inwardly at the slight Dianne's so-called husband had given them, and Dianne was confused. There were no easy answers to her many questions, and so it seemed that the surface conversation was the only way to brush over that which she could not set right.

When it came time for the Todds to leave, Mary-Ann was genuine in her gratitude, but it was all she could do to hold back from adding some indignant remark concerning the earlier incident. Peter's words were so gentle and reassuring that Dianne was almost ready to accept that the evening had been a success.

"I will be over again soon," he added quietly. "Don't be surprised to see me!"

Dianne nodded, understanding his purpose, and feeling deeply grateful that he was going to take it upon himself to break through the barrier of loneliness that surrounded her husband.

Dianne tucked Jillian in her bed. It had been a big experience for the little girl which had tired her out, so she fell asleep straight away. Having kissed Jillian's forehead, Dianne smiled as she watched the pretty little face sleeping peacefully. She felt so pleased with how much the two of them had learned, and exceptionally pleased that Jillian had met and interacted easily with the Todds.

All the cleaning up was finished and the doors locked and Dianne was thinking about going to her bed in the small cluttered office, but her heart was troubled over the incident with Richard. She sighed with frustration knowing there was little she could do to change anything, and she took up the kerosene lamp to light her room.

She had just let her hair down and had started to pull the brush through its length, pretending as she did so that she could brush away the tension with each stroke of the brush, when she was startled by a knock at the door of her room. Carefully, she put the brush down and moved quietly to the door, half afraid that her imagination was playing tricks on her.

"Here!" Richard thrust a piece of paper toward her, the moment she'd opened the door.

"What's this?" Dianne asked, startled.

"It's proof, all right!" His voice was marked with bitterness and anger. "Read it, Dianne, and then you can be satisfied!"

Dianne looked down at the paper but the light was dim and she couldn't make out what the writing was all about. She stepped back into her room, and moved closer to the lamp before beginning to read.

"So, you see!" Richard said to her from the hall. "I didn't strangle her, or poison her one stormy night. See! It's written there that the cause of death was tuberculosis, and look, Dianne, she wasn't even here at the time!"

Dianne could indeed see that what she held was the certificate of death of Mrs. Helen Schrouder, and she was stunned at the suddenness with which the information had been revealed. She was also a little chagrined, but didn't admit to Richard that she *had*, at one time, thought some sinister thoughts about how this woman had died.

"Are you happy now?" Richard continued defensively.

"But why, Richard?" Dianne turned back toward him, a question in her eyes. "Why do you have to show all this to me?"

"Don't think that I don't know what you've been thinking." Dianne failed to hide a blush, as if he'd read her earlier thought. "I know what everybody has said about her. The little children have very informative tongues, you know!"

"But I didn't seriously think that you'd done away with you wife, Richard." Dianne hastened to assure him.

"What did you think, then, Mrs. Pierceson?" Richard seemed to be caught in mounting bitterness, and it seemed as if he was deliberately trying to be cutting.

"If you are trying to shame me by using my former husband's name, Mr. Schrouder, I'll have you know that my husband, Samuel, was a fine upstanding man, and I will never ever be ashamed of his name or his memory. I only wonder if the same can be said of your dead wife!"

As soon as the harsh words had left her mouth, Dianne put her hand over her mouth, regretting having said them. She was momentarily afraid that she had provoked a sleeping giant, remembering the glimpse of deep rage from her first uninvited visit to his house. Richard saw her flinch, as if to avoid being struck.

"Do you think I'm a wife beater?" he demanded, suddenly alert to a new possibility.

"I don't know what am I supposed to think?" she shot back, still on guard.

"I never struck her, not once!" His voice was suddenly no longer furious, and he sounded utterly weary.

"I never said you beat your wife, Richard," Dianne said quietly.

"Yes, but there was that time I was too rough with you." He searched her face and could see she remembered the day she'd discovered Jillian.

"You see, you remember too. When I saw you, I lost all sense of reason. For those few moments I felt overcome with rage. I've never felt like that before, and I hope I never do again. I'm sorry for what I did. You don't know how sorry."

Dianne looked on silently.

"I have never physically harmed either my wife or my daughter. I loved them both - very much - until...." He broke off with a sigh, and he hung his head as if the weight of the memory was too much. Yet he made no move to retreat.

"What do you want from me?" Dianne asked, her own voice shakey with emotion.

"I want you to believe in me, Dianne. I'm not the monster that Mrs Todd has described me as. Oh! I know that I appear hostile and unfriendly, but inside, I never wanted her to leave."

Dianne heard the defeat in his tone, and waited again, unsure as to whether she should prompt him for more information, or whether she should just bid him 'good-night'; but neither action was necessary.

"She was very sick when Jillian was still small," he continued, obviously wishing to get the story off his chest. "I didn't know what was wrong with her at the time, only that the doctor had prescribed that she be admitted to an institution in the city. At first I could not leave the school, and it was hard with the baby and all, but when I finally got away, after leaving the baby with Reverend Andrews and his wife, Helen refused to see me. I was left standing in the hall of the hospital. I didn't know she was dying. I didn't know why she wouldn't see me. All I knew was that my pride had been hurt, and I foolishly vowed that I wouldn't make another effort to contact her. Within the year she was dead, and all I knew about it was that death certificate sent to me in the mail."

Dianne's heart was wrung with sympathy, and yet still there was nothing she could do. His past was full of unresolved issues, and she didn't have the first idea of how she could help him work through them.

Moments passed and the atmosphere remained strained as Richard made no attempt to leave.

"Thank you for telling me, Richard," Dianne suddenly spoke, not knowing what else to do. "I'm sorry too. I didn't understand about Jillian or your wife, but I thank you for sharing it with me, and thank you for allowing me to have guests here. It meant a lot to me!"

He lifted his head to look at her. "I'm sorry, Dianne, sorry that I was rude to your guests." He paused for a few moments, as if gathering courage to go on. "Next time, I will be more civil!"

Dianne smiled as she realized that he had given his permission for her to try her plan again.

"You'd best go to bed," she urged. "Tomorrow is another day!"

He turned away obediently, but Dianne could not help but think that it was reluctantly.

Chapter Seventeen

Dianne had sensed a difference in the way she and Richard related after that evening. He had lowered his guard with her to some degree. She had caught a glimpse of how he'd felt about his former wife. But there was still a lot she didn't know, and while she was glad that he seemed less hard, she still didn't want to go blundering in with a lot of insensitive questions. Apart from anything else, if Richard should choose to become open and vulnerable, she didn't know whether she would be able to handle the complexities that were certain to come with it. So she kept their relationship on an even level, not quite as impersonal as it had been, but certainly not intimate. For the first time in the nine months since they married, she actually felt as if she was settled in her position. She not only enjoyed teaching Jillian, and showing her all about life, she actually felt she loved the little girl. And she felt that she respected Richard enough to care about him.

One weekday afternoon, Dianne was surprised by Richard appearing at the back door and calling her name. She had been sweeping the porch and was not expecting him to come in until later in the afternoon, after the children were let out. He immediately asked her if she would come around to the classroom and sit with the children for a while.

"What's the matter?" she asked, puzzled.

"There's something wrong at the Jansen household," he said quickly. "Kenny has been absent for over a week, and Ted's excuses are becoming unbelievable. I just want to go over and check on things for myself; just to make sure the little fellow is all right."

"But, what about Jillian?"

"Will she come with you?" Richard asked.

"I don't think she will, not without a lot of coaxing, at least. I haven't tried taking her out of the house yet."

Richard seemed disappointed, and so Dianne went on. "How much time do you have?"

"I guess I don't have to rush over there," he replied. "See if you can get her to come with you."

Dianne put the broom away and began to plan just how she would convince Jillian to follow her outside of the house. Jillian's skills in communication had increased so dramatically that it wasn't as hard to make her intentions known as Dianne had thought. She responded in a manner that indicated she very much wanted to please her stepmother, despite evident anxiety. Dianne could tell that Jillian had been wondering about the outside world, and yet she recognised there was still a lot of apprehension about actually stepping outside the familiar environment that had been her whole world.

Methodically and calmly Dianne signed to her that it was her father who wanted them to come, and reassured her, using the now familiar signs of "LOVE" and "FRIENDS", that there would be other new people to meet.

It soon became obvious just how much the little girl had grown to trust her teacher-parent. Jillian took Dianne's hand and led her toward the back door, as if to say that she was ready to try this new venture, and face the unknown.

Richard was both surprised and pleased to see Dianne enter the classroom door leading his eleven-year-old daughter by the hand. He quickly explained the situation to the other children in the classroom.

"You will remember I have spoken to you about my daughter, Jillian," he began. "And of course you will remember that I told you that my daughter is deaf. She cannot hear at all. You all remember Mrs. Pierceson. She is now my wife, and so you may address her as Mrs. Schrouder. She has come in to see you all today, and has brought my daughter, Jillian, to spend some special time with you. This afternoon Mrs. Schrouder will give you a lesson in using sign language which people who cannot hear use to communicate."

Dianne hadn't really thought about what she would do when she got to the classroom. Her whole attention had been focussed on gaining enough of Jillian's trust to actually get her here, and now as she heard Richard outline the plans, she was quite taken aback. To hear him speak, it sounded as if they had discussed it fully and planned for the lesson to be this way all along. She was on the spot now, but felt equal to the task and wasted no time in taking charge of the group of children.

While the school pupils were clearly displaying their curiosity at seeing both a girl who was deaf and their former school teacher, Dianne also took careful note of Jillian's response to this new situation. She could see by the look on the child's face that she was enthralled to see so many "FRIENDS" who were the same size as herself. She could also sense Jillian's apprehension, and made sure that she used all of the signs available to reassure and encourage her.

It didn't take very long before Jillian felt comfortable enough to sit down on a chair next to her at the front of the class.

Richard watched just long enough to reassure himself that everything was going to be all right. As he hurried down the street towards the Jansens' house, he hoped that the school children would respond positively to the lesson that he was sure Dianne would teach them. He recognised that it had taken him nearly eleven years to learn this lesson, and at times he still mentally berated himself at having been so ignorant, and having caused such unnecessary cruelty.

As he walked he had to battle with his own thoughts. Self-condemnation had been a constant companion for too many years, and it was easy for him to let that dark cloud settle on his mind. But Dianne's optimism and her success with his daughter had shaken some of the grip that particular gloom had on his thoughts, and he began to allow some of his natural intelligence and logic to work; to plead a different case in his mind. What he'd done he'd done, and there was nothing he could do to change it, but he recognised he could change the future, if only he would push past the barrier of self-doubt that had been keeping him from achieving any great purpose.

Even the situation with Kenny Jansen had been Dianne's success. There was another stab of self-accusation that he had to chase away. He'd misjudged that situation and not acted soon enough, but now he wanted to try with all his influence to see if there wasn't something to be done to help the boy.

The full ten-minute walk to the Jansen home, right through to the other side of the town, was taken up with his own particular brand of self-talk. The pleasant afternoon sunshine was wasted on Richard as he focussed his thoughts on Kenny's situation. His older brother Ted had told him the bare facts without any elaboration. Richard had developed the concern he felt from what he believed Ted had *not* said.

As Richard approached the Jansen home, he was not surprised to see it in a state of disrepair, even though the garden was neatly kept. Richard knew that the tidy lawns and flower beds were due largely to the efforts of the older son, Ted. It wasn't just that Ted had told him this himself, but a number of gossiping parents had made comment over the disgraceful habits of Mr and Mrs Jansen.

Mentally preparing himself, Richard walked up the path towards the front door, with confident outward bearing, yet inside anxious as to what he might discover. For a few moments, he was assailed again by feelings of guilt. In times past, Richard had failed to call on any of the children's parents. It had been years, in fact, during which time the headmaster had hidden behind his own family trials, and had made excuses to himself as to why it was all right to withdraw from the community. Now he had to admit that in this also he had been wrong. But he also recognised that now was not the time to be going over his own failures and faults. He had a job to do, and it was time he faced up to this neglected responsibility.

"What d'ya want?" A harsh female voice growled through the wire screen door.

"I've come to inquire after Kenny, Mrs. Jansen," Richard spoke failing to hide his anxiety.

"Didn't Ted tell ya he was sick?" she answered bluntly. "Cursed boy, never does anything he's told!"

"Ted delivered the message, ma'am. I just thought Kenny might appreciate a visit from his teacher, some encouragement when he's not well!" The inspiration for words flowed better now that the conversation was under way.

"We don't want none of your kind snooping around here, Mr. Schrouder. Kenny's doin' just fine without your interference, thank you very much!"

Richard knew that he could not force his way past the hostile mother, and so he was obliged to tip his hat and turn around having relieved none of the fears he had felt about Kenny's welfare.

Once again the self-recriminations rose up to accuse him. He strongly regretted having cut himself off to such an extent that town gossip was as much against him as it was against the Jansens. He knew he had lost all credibility amongst the townspeople, but there was little he could do to change that fact.

Just as he was about to open the front gate and step back onto the footpath, he heard a young voice calling his name, and though it was soft, he definitely heard it. He turned to see who it was, already guessing that it was Kenny. He was hiding behind the side of the house, waving to his schoolmaster to come to him. Richard immediately turned back and hurried to where Kenny was hiding. He was momentarily thankful that he'd been given the opportunity to speak with the boy who seemed to have forgiven him for misunderstanding him. But when he was close enough to see Kenny's face, Richard was halted in his tracks. A boiling anger rose from within as he saw his little face, swollen and black with bruises. As Richard looked closer at him, he could see that Kenny's legs were also bruised.

"Kenny! Are you all right?"

"Please don't be angry with me, Sir," the boy stuttered. "I want to come back to school, but my mother won't let me go."

"I'm not angry, Kenny." Richard suppressed from his tone the anger he'd felt, and allowed his true sympathy to show. "What happened to you?"

The boy hung his head in silence. Suddenly Richard remembered the times he'd tried to get Kenny to obey using threats of punishment, and the surge of guilt almost choked him. Dianne had recognised it almost at once, but he had been so caught up in his own problems that he had blundered on, possibly causing more damage. It took a mammoth effort, but Richard was determined to right some of his own wrongs, and so he swallowed his own worries. He knelt down so as to be at eye level with the boy, and hoped he didn't appear threatening.

"It's all right to tell me, Kenny. Don't be afraid." Richard coaxed.

"He fell off his bike, all right, Schrouder!" Mr Jansen's booming voice broke from behind Kenny, and Richard looked up to see the boy's father standing over him. Immediately Kenny's eyes lit with panic, and he began to tremble and whimper.

"Shut-up, boy," the father spoke harshly, "or I'll clout you one!"

"I'm afraid you've already 'clouted' him once too many times." Richard stood up and spoke boldly. "I don't believe Kenny fell off his bike, or had any other normal mishap. I believe that these bruises are a result of your beating the boy."

"What if they are, teacher?" Edward Jansen bit back. "You're known to hit the kids yourself, now and again!"

"Never to the point of harm, sir." Richard hotly defended the truth. "Occasionally as a punishment I administer the cane, but you will never see bruises of any kind, let alone bruises like this!" He pointed toward the frightened child.

"Come off it, mate," Jansen continued. "You know what a difficult child Kenny is. I've heard how many times you've had to give him the cuts."

"Kenny would you go inside to your mother." Richard was very aware of the small child standing in between them, and that he must be feeling very threatened by the aggressive conversation. But Kenny didn't move. His father had his hand on his shoulder.

"I've adjusted my discipline with Kenny," Richard went on. "It would appear you are being too heavy-handed with him, and it is affecting him."

"Don't you come here telling me how I should treat my own kids, Schrouder. Talk is you've not done so well with your own daughter!"

Richard's anger began to rise, and it was apparent.

"Yes! You see. We've all heard about your temper, so I wouldn't go around preaching to others, if I were you." Edward sounded smug.

"Whatever you have heard, Mr. Jansen," Richard calculated his words, "you will never have heard that I have physically harmed anyone, and certainly not to the extent that I see here."

"No-one asked you to come snooping around here." Edward maintained his bravado. "This is my property and Kenny's my kid. How I treat him is my business."

Richard knew that according to law this was true, but his peripheral vision told him that Kenny was cowering in terror under his father's hand. In all his days of administering discipline he had never seen such abject terror, and his heart melted at the sight of it.

"I am going to take Kenny with me!" He suddenly announced, and didn't wait for the father to respond. He just bent forward, picked up the frail child, and began to walk away.

"You put him down, Schrouder," the father yelled. "I'll have you up on charges of kidnap so fast you won't know what hit you!"

Richard ignored the threats and continued to carry the trembling boy away from his angry father.

☆ ☆ ☆ ☆

"But you can't just take a child away from his parents," Dianne argued, once she'd listened to Richard's story.

"Technically, no I can't, Dianne, but I have, and there's nothing to be done about it now!" Richard's voice was firm and resolute.

"What are you going to do if the father brings charges of kidnap against you?" Dianne sounded almost desperate.

"He won't," Richard assured. "If he brings the law into it, he's going to have to start explaining the bruises all over Kenny's body."

Dianne turned back to her dishes, upset over the whole unfortunate affair.

"Doctor Stewart is considering whether Kenny should be sent to the city for hospital treatment, anyway. It's out of my hands now."

When Dianne made no answer for quite a while, Richard decided to pursue the conversation.

"You think I've made the wrong decision?"

"I don't know," she answered honestly. "It's like something I don't want to have to face."

"I couldn't ignore it, Dianne. The child was black and blue with bruises."

"I know," she answered quietly.

"I've made so many mistakes in the past, I think it's high time I started to take some positive action, don't you?"

"I think you are doing really well, Richard," Dianne said genuinely. "You and Jillian are relating now, and...well, you've always done well in the classroom."

"Except with Kenny!"

"You didn't understand the situation."

"I should've understood. I should have seen it."

"But it's much better now, isn't it? You've made the changes."

He held her gaze for a few moments after she'd finsished speaking. Suddenly, Dianne broke the contact and he realised what had been passing between them. There had been genuine emotion in her look, at least a deep caring, if not something deeper. Richard was disappointed as he got up from the table, sorry that the exchange had broken. As he began to move out of the kitchen, he spoke to her.

"You have been the only one who has been able to set me straight when I've been wrong," he said evenly. "I don't know what I would do without you!"

Dianne heard what he said and stood still a moment, shocked by what she understood. She shook her head, not wanting to accept what he actually meant. Each day, she was coming to understand her husband more, and with the passing of time, she began to realise that he was beginning to have feelings for her – real, undisguised affection. It was a realisation that horrified her. This had never been part of the bargain. Dianne had not looked for love in this marriage, only provision. And Richard had provided for her, and in return, Dianne had looked after the house, and his daughter. But what she had failed to factor into the equation was the fact that she had opened up the world of relationship to him again. She had taught him to communicate with his daughter; she had helped him to understand students like Kenny, and she had re-introduced him to a friend and mentor in Peter Todd. Richard's self-imposed personal isolation was gone, and it was Dianne who had done it. He was beginning to feel again, and she had become aware that he was beginning to feel something deep for her. She didn't think she was ready for that. She didn't know if she would ever be ready for it. The only solution was for her to try and avoid keeping company with him.

Chapter Eighteen

Dianne was still up sewing by lamplight long after the others had gone to bed. She often had so many thoughts buzzing around in her mind she couldn't sleep, and she found that applying herself to some task often helped clear her mind sooner.

She was startled from those thoughts by a loud banging on the back door. Surprised, she looked up from her sewing. Picking up the table lamp she moved slowly toward the back porch, all the time wondering who it would be knocking at this late hour, and with such fierce determination.

"Who's there?" she called through the wooden door.

"Open up this door," a gruff voice yelled back. "I want my boy back, and I want him now!"

"Mr. Jansen?"

"Open up, or I'll break the door down!"

Dianne's alarm grew as she heard some foul language added to this threat.

"Kenny's not here, Mr. Jansen," Dianne said quickly.

"I know he's in there. That schoolmaster took him from right under my nose."

"Mr. Schrouder has taken Kenny to Doctor Stewart's house. The doctor is treating your son!"

Though this was the truth, Edward Jansen obviously didn't believe it, and Dianne jumped back from the door as it rattled under the strain of having been thumped by Edward's full body weight, shoulder to the door.

The door rattled again under the strain of a second blow, and Dianne could see that the flimsy lock would not hold the intruder at bay for much longer.

Without thinking she put the lamp down on the porch floor, and fled down the hall towards her husband's bedroom. The hallway was dark and in her panic she did not see that Richard was already awake and coming towards her down the hall. Without warning Dianne crashed headlong into his strong body. With the advantage of the dim light glowing behind her, Richard was able to catch her and prevent her from falling.

"What's wrong?" he demanded, very concerned. "What's all that noise about?"

"Kenny's father is trying to break down the back door." Dianne spoke breathlessly. "He sounds as if he's drunk."

"You wait here," Richard said, then released her and moved swiftly to the back porch. Jansen was still attempting to push the door down with his shoulder, but Richard was not perturbed. He quickly unlocked the door, and faced the angry father on his doorstep.

"Where's my boy, schoolmaster?" Edward Jansen demanded when he saw Richard. "I want him now!"

"He's not here, Mr. Jansen." Richard's voice was controlled and even.

"So I've already heard! Who's she, anyway?" Jansen was drunk and his talk bold and direct as he referred to Dianne, who was not waiting in the hall, but standing timidly a few steps behind her husband. "Is she a new mistress, or someone else's wife, this time?"

Richard felt the deliberate insult and was angered by it. Dianne could see that he was beginning to lose his calm.

"Richard! Don't listen to him!" she cried out as she saw the potential for a fight. "Let him go. It doesn't matter what he says!"

"Go back inside, Dianne," he ordered firmly. "I'll just see Mr. Jansen from the property."

Dianne backed into the lounge room, too afraid to turn her back on the hostile scene in the back porch. She sat down but her body was tense and her heart was racing.

She waited patiently for what seemed like a long time, straining to hear the sound of Richard returning indoors, but no such sound reached her ears. At first she reasoned that Richard must have been trying to talk reason to the aggrieved father, and these thoughts kept her seated for a further ten minutes. But after nearly half an hour with still no sign of his return, Dianne began to panic. She could not make up her mind whether she should go to investigate or not.

Eventually her own reason would not allow her to sit still. There had been plenty of time for Richard to have talked Edward Jansen around, but still he had not returned. Summoning all her courage, Dianne picked up the lamp and cautiously ventured outside. She didn't call out for fear of attracting attention, but she did hold the lamp up high to light the immediate area in which she walked. She followed the path around the house to the front garden, all the while carefully scanning the bushes and trees, half afraid that someone would jump out from behind one of them.

Her stomach knotted up as the anxiety mounted with each step she took, and still there was no sign of her missing husband. It wasn't until she reached the front of the house that she saw him sprawled across the garden path.

"Richard!" she cried as she hurried over to discover why he lay so still. Setting the lamp down next to him she immediately searched for a pulse, and breathed a sigh of relief when she found one pumping steadily in his neck.

"What's happened?" she asked, almost expecting him to open his eyes and answer, but there was no response whatever.

Dianne stood up, picked up the lamp and hurried across the road to the Todds. Her feelings were in turmoil. The large gash on the side of Richard's head had shocked her, and added to an avalanche of other unidentified emotions. She didn't have the time or presence of mind to recognise what she really felt.

"He's bleeding," she sobbed helplessly, once she saw Peter Todd standing in his doorway. "I think he's dying, Mr. Todd. Hurry, please!"

"Where is he?" Peter asked immediately.

Dianne pointed back toward the school house. "He's lying on the footpath at the front of the house."

Peter didn't even wait to go back and change from his pyjamas. With slippered feet, he raced across to the schoolhouse.

By this time, Mary-Ann had emerged from the bedroom, buttoning her own dressing gown. The moment Dianne saw her, she broke down in a fit of crying.

"I didn't know what to do," she cried. "What if he dies, Mrs Todd. What will happen?"

"There, there, love," Mary-Ann comforted her. "Peter will set things to right. You'd best sit down, and I'd best go for the doctor. I'll make you a cup of tea when I get back."

Dianne nodded, understanding that they needed to act quickly, and wiping her eyes she began to bring her emotions back under control.

"I'd better go back home, Mrs. Todd," she said, a little more calmly. "Jillian is all alone!"

Mary-Ann nodded in agreement. "I'll walk you across, dear," she offered kindly.

Some hour and a half later, Dianne was in the lounge room, staring at the prescribed cup of tea, but not able to bring herself to drink it. Peter had waited for the doctor before attempting to move Richard. He was quite a large man, and was still unconscious. Even with the doctor's assistance, it was not easy getting him inside.

Doctor Stewart and Peter Todd had been in the end room with her injured husband for what seemed like an eternity. Still Dianne could not bring herself to face her own feelings. She easily recognised her panic and then her worry, but there was a whole range of other emotions that seemed vaguely familiar, emotions that Dianne felt had been a part of her relationship with Samuel, and yet it was Richard who was injured, perhaps dying. The whole ordeal was overwhelming.

She did not know how long she had sat gazing blankly into space before she'd nodded off. All she knew was that she found herself waking up in her own bed, the sun already high in the sky.

Instantly, she recalled the night before with all the worry and fear that had tormented her before nodding off. With renewed energy, she got straight out of bed, and took a few moments to straighten her hair. She was still dressed in the clothes she'd had on the previous evening.

"Are you all right, love?" Mary-Ann greeted Dianne the moment she stepped out of her office-bedroom.

"What's happened, Mrs. Todd?" Dianne couldn't hide her fear and anxiety. "Is the doctor still here?"

"No, dear. He's left about three o'clock in the morning." The older woman was calm and reassuring.

"And Richard? Is he....?" She couldn't bring herself to ask the awful question.

"He's alive, Dianne, although still unconscious. The doctor doesn't know the extent of damage the injury has caused."

Dianne breathed an audible sigh of relief.

"He's not out of danger yet, dear," Mary-Ann cautioned. "Head injuries can turn on you at any moment, as I understand it!"

Dianne studied Mrs Todd's face, looking for signs of reassurance. The capable woman did seem quite confident, but Dianne had heard what she'd said about head injuries. She recalled that Samuel's accident had involved a bleeding in the brain, and she knew only too well how that had ended. The knowledge was no comfort at all, and quite suddenly, Dianne was faced with the reality that she did feel something for Richard after all. But she still didn't know what to do with these feelings. She wasn't even sure that they were right.

"Do you want to see him?" Mary-Ann asked, breaking into her thoughts. "Doctor Stewart said it will be all right for you to sit with him."

"No!" Dianne burst out, perhaps a little too quickly. "Just so long as the doctor has seen he is all right."

"What about the little girl?" Mary-Ann asked, just a little puzzled. "She was quite upset when I went in earlier. She obviously doesn't understand what's happened!"

"Jillian!" Dianne immediately looked up, ashamed that in her anxiety, she had completely forgotten about the little girl. "Where is she?"

"She's hiding under her bed. I couldn't make her come out. I did try." Mary-Ann said with some regret.

"Oh no!" Dianne groaned. "She must be really frightened to have gone back there!"

Dianne went directly to Jillian's room, a thousand thoughts tumbling about in her mind as to how she might communicate the news of the accident to the frightened child.

Jillian brightened the moment she saw Dianne, and instantly came out from her hiding place, quickly crossing the room to receive the embrace to which she'd become accustomed.

"Oh, little Jill," Dianne whispered. "Whatever will you do if he dies?"

Of course Jillian couldn't hear Dianne's words, but she immediately sensed her distress, and pulled back from her to study her face for clues. The child's dark eyes, so much like her father's, looked deep into Dianne's soul, so much so that Dianne was unnerved, as if the child had actually asked a direct question for which she had no answer.

"What am I supposed to do?" Dianne asked aloud, though there was no-one to answer her. "How ever will I make her understand?"

"FATHER" Jillian signed, obviously sensing that something was wrong with him, and wanting an explanation.

"FATHER - SICK" Dianne signed in return, but Jillian only looked at her blankly. There had never been an occasion to use the sign describing illness and Jillian didn't understand what the sign was related to.

"Come with me, Jillian," Dianne spoke as she took the child by the hand and led her toward her father's bedroom.

The curtains were partially drawn, making the room almost dark and the atmosphere seem unnatural. In bringing Jillian to her father's bedside, Dianne had forgotten her own feelings for a moment, and was now quite shocked to see the man who was her legal husband lying deathly still, his features pale and unresponsive. For just a moment Dianne panicked as she imagined that he was already dead, but she reached out and touched his warm forehead, and noted that his chest was still rising and falling. Relief washed over her as she recognised the signs of life.

But Jillian had no idea what these signs meant, or indeed what had happened to her father in the first place to make him lie so still and unresponsive. She was obviously shocked and troubled, and began to whimper. Instantly Dianne turned to the child, and realised what she was feeling. She put her arm about the little girl's shoulders to comfort her.

"Please, dear Lord," she prayed quietly. "Don't let him die. For Jillian's sake, I pray, let him live!"

Eventually, she released the child, and began to sign to her.

"FATHER - SICK" Dianne signed.

Jillian nodded in understanding, but her eyes did not light up with the usual excitement of a new word learned. She looked sadly at her father. Though she had seen him all her life, it was only just recently that he'd become a friend to her through the communication Dianne had taught them both.

"LOVE - FATHER" Dianne prompted the daughter.

Jillian held back apprehensively, unsure of what was expected of her.

"LOVE - FATHER" Dianne encouraged, demonstrating further by smoothing her hand across the unconscious man's cheek. She reached out for Jillian, to prompt her to do the same, expressing her love by touch. Eventually, she followed her teacher's example and reached out her small hand to touch her father's face. Tears sprang to her eyes, and Dianne couldn't help but cry too at seeing just how much Richard's sickness had affected his little girl.

Chapter Nineteen

Dianne did not return to the sickroom again. She knew that Jillian spent most of her time by her father's side, holding his hand and brushing any straying hair back to its proper place. But Dianne was plagued by feelings of ambivalance. She didn't feel as if it were her place to be so intimate. She knew now that she had strong underlying feelings about Richard, but she just wasn't sure about how he felt about her. She had sensed that he was growing in his affections for her, but he had never said anything in plain words that could mark a change in their relationship from work associates to intimate husband and wife. And to complicate the issue for Dianne, there were the other feelings of being unfaithful to her first husband's memory. Dianne was quite troubled over the situation and felt that to distance herself from Richard's bedroom was the safest way while there were no answers to be had. And she justified this further by telling herself that as she was taking full responsibility of the school all her time and energy were fully engaged.

Mary-Ann Todd offered to stay on in the household while Dianne worked in the classroom. She would have loved to go back to teaching if it hadn't been under such trying circumstances. As it was, she had to work with all her might to appear at ease and in charge. All the children were troubled over their schoolmaster's illness and constantly asked Dianne for a report on his recovery. But she didn't have any good news to report and so led them in daily prayer as much for her own peace of mind as that of the students.

Doctor Stewart returned Kenny to his home, and shortly after, the little boy started coming back to school. Dianne did not know the full details of what had eventuated, but it was rumoured that Doctor Stewart had spoken seriously to Kenny's parents, and that a warning had been issued should any more signs of bruising appear. Bearing all this in mind, Dianne kept a close watch on Kenny, monitoring his responses, and looking carefully for any signs of physical abuse. She had been deeply troubled by the whole situation surrounding this little boy, and she hated the thought that he might have to live his whole childhood suffering cruel beatings.

Peter Todd had made regular visits to the schoolmaster's house, coming across daily after he'd finished helping his son on the farm. He'd talked to Dianne extensively regarding the circumstances surrounding the so-called accident. At first she had been reluctant to mention the fact that Mr Jansen had been threatening them, since she was at home alone and unprotected, save for a small child and unconscious husband, but eventually she had to tell Peter about him being there angry and drunk.

Despite this information, however, there was never any other evidence to suggest that anything had happened other than an unfortunate accident. Some serious questions were raised as to how it was that Mr Jansen hadn't raised the alarm once Richard had fallen, but he maintained that he knew nothing of the accident, and that it must have happened after he'd left. And he didn't make any secret about the fact that it was what he felt the schoolmaster deserved.

Peter didn't mention any of this to Dianne, however. Only that there wouldn't be any police investigation into the matter.

As time passed, it became apparent that Richard's condition had stabilised and that he wasn't going to die, yet he remained in a coma. The tension and worry were a constant weight, not only on Dianne's mind, but on all those who waited for Richard to regain consciousness. It wasn't just the anxiety of wanting to know what actually happened, or even that the school and family needed Richard healthy and active, but there was also the unspoken worry that he might never rouse and might remain in a vegetative state. This was a heavy burden to carry.

It had been over two weeks of such tension before Dianne was summoned by the doctor.

"Mrs. Schrouder," he began quietly. "I think it's only wise to warn you that if your husband does regain consciousness, and there is still some doubt as to whether he will, I don't want you to expect too much."

Dianne looked blankly at Doctor Stewart, not really understanding what he was saying.

"There is every chance that your husband may have sustained permanent brain damage." He could see she didn't fully understand, and knew it was his responsibility to spell it out for her, though it was not an easy thing to say. "No-one can say at this stage if there is any permanent damage or not, or even what nature it could take if there is."

Dianne's heart sank further with despair and confusion. She had prayed for Richard's life to be spared, and yet, if it was only to reward him with being a cripple or even mentally handicapped she didn't know if she would be able to cope with such a burden, or even how he himself would cope.

Peter and Mary-Ann had heard the doctor's report and immediately sensed the depression that had settled over their young friend. They were very concerned to see her withdraw, not only from the comatose patient, but also from Jillian.

"I think it is time to call in Mr Andrews," Mary-Ann suggested to her husband, one day. "Dianne is not coping at all well with the family situation as it is!"

Peter agreed and took it upon himself to arrange for the minister to come and speak with Dianne the very next Saturday.

"How is your husband progressing?" Mr Andrews enquired in a kindly manner.

"Doctor Stewart is uncertain as to the extent of damage - even uncertain as to whether he will live or not. Nobody can really say, at this point." Dianne spoke what she knew as one reciting unimportant information.

"Have you noticed any sign of recognition, Mrs. Schrouder?" he asked. "I mean, I have heard that often a coma victim will try to signal his ability to comprehend, over and above the unconsciousness!"

Dianne didn't reply, only cast her eyes down in the usual way she did when she felt ashamed.

"What's the matter?" The minister perceived that something was wrong, and asked the question gently. "Hasn't he shown you any sign of recognition?"

Tears began to well in her eyes as the stress and guilt began to overcome her.

"I haven't seen him!" Dianne said quietly, tears beginning to roll from the corners of her eyes.

Compassionately, the pastor remained quiet for some time, trying to process what she was saying. But his silence unnerved her, and Dianne began to feel an obligation to justify her position.

"He's not really my husband, Reverend Andrews," she stammered. "We have no real relationship. We never have had!"

"I knew that it was a matter of convenience when you approached me to marry you, but I had thought that perhaps, after this time, you might have begun to grow closer together."

Dianne shook her head. "We have never talked about it," she said quickly, "and even if we had, I don't feel right about it. I'm not really a part of his life to be caring about him in such a deep way!"

"I don't understand what you're saying, Mrs. Schrouder," he prompted.

"I already have a husband," she cried recklessly, "and I love him very much!"

"I beg your pardon!" The minister sounded shocked. "I hope I've misunderstood what you're saying. It is against the law to be married to more than one man at the same time. Why didn't you inform me of this before, when I asked you if there was any reason why you and Richard should not be married?"

"My first husband is dead," Dianne spoke sadly.

The minister sighed with relief.

"But he is as much a part of me now as when he was alive," Dianne hastened to explain.

"Mrs. Schrouder," the minister began patiently. "Who do you live with?"

"Richard," she answered meekly.

"And who provides for your needs, and protects you?"

"Richard!"

"And who is it that loves and cares about you?"

"No!" Dianne screamed in rebellion at the thought. "Samuel loved me very much, and he cared about me more than you could believe. I can't turn my back on him!"

"But Samuel Pierceson is dead, Mrs. Schrouder. How can he love you and care about you when he is dead?"

"But he would, if only he was alive," she argued, stubbornly refusing to yield to his reason.

"But he's not alive, is he?" He held her gaze firmly. "Is he, Dianne?"

"No!" She broke down in a flood of tears, her pent up grief finally releasing itself.

"Richard Schrouder is alive, Dianne, and he loves you, and cares about you. You know that, don't you?"

She nodded through the blinding tears.

"And right now he needs you more than he's ever needed anyone before!"

"But I feel so guilty, Reverend," Dianne wiped at her eyes. "I feel as if I have been unfaithful to Samuel."

"Dianne!" The minister's words were full of sympathy. "Your late husband is now gone to his reward. He resides with his Lord, Jesus Christ, and he no longer has any part of this life; but if there were any connection between here and there, and if he could know of your situation, wouldn't he want you to be happy and fulfilled in this life? I speak of the Samuel that you knew."

"He would want me to be happy," Dianne confirmed reluctantly.

"What is going to make you happy? Do you want to divorce Richard Schrouder? Then you can live with the memories of your past!" He searched her face for a response, forcing her to face the question. "Do you?" he persisted.

"No!" she admitted quietly. "I don't want a divorce!"

"Well, what do you want?"

There was a long pause as Dianne struggled with the question. Reverend Andrews continued to regard her steadfastly, and though she didn't look up into his face, she knew that he was waiting for her to answer. Finally it all came to the surface in a rush.

"I want you to tell me that it's all right to love Richard Schrouder. I want so much to love him, but I want you to tell me that it's not wrong. I'm so scared to let go in case it is wrong!" Dianne's voice cracked with emotion as she finally released those feelings that had been simmering beneath the surface for many weeks.

"It would be wrong, Dianne, for you not to love him, especially with all he has faced, and all he may have to face. He needs you desperately. You are his lawful wedded wife, and he needs you more than ever, to love and care for him!"

The tears flowed unchecked, and even the minister reached up to wipe the corner of his eyes.

"Come with me, Dianne," he urged, standing up from his chair. "We will go together and pray for your husband!"

The minister placed his hand on her shoulder, and drew her forward which seemed to give Dianne the courage she needed. The Reverend Andrews had reassured her that it was not only all right, but it was necessary that she allow herself to love her husband, Richard Schrouder. She had been wanting to acknowledge these feelings for some time, but had stifled them, and pushed them away as something she couldn't or shouldn't face.

Now, walking into Richard's bedroom, it was the enemy inside her own mind that she needed to face. As she saw her husband looking much the same as he had when she'd left those many days ago, her heart broke over again.

"Go on," the minister urged. "Go to him, and tell him."

It was no use trying to withhold tears, but time to let go, and they came easily. She knelt down next to him and took hold of his hand.

"Richard." She found it nearly impossible to speak over the lump of emotion in her throat. She paused a moment, and swallowed hard to regain some form of control.

"Richard," she said again. "I'm sorry, love. I'm sorry I haven't been here for you. I love you, and I want to be with you. Please get well. Please. I need you."

The emotion was like a wave that threatened to overwhelm, and she broke down, placing her head against his chest and crying her heart out. But the only response she received was the gentle rising and falling of his chest, and she could hear the steady beating of his heart. It was life, and that was all that she could hope for at this point.

Chapter Twenty

There were those who continued to visit the comatose schoolmaster. Doctor Stewart persisted in shaking his head in despair each time he checked Richard's progress. Peter Todd habitually sat and talked to the patient, chatting as if he were awake and well, fully able to respond. On several occasions he had brought his wife in to mumble a greeting and a few words of encouragement. This small act of kindness had gone sorely against her grain, but Peter's wishes were obeyed, especially in the light of Dianne's apparent commitment and new hope for her husband.

The Reverend Andrews made it his business to call regularly. He prayed and talked to Richard, in much the same way as Peter Todd. The doctor had agreed that it was quite possible the patient could hear, even though he was unable to respond, and that their friendly one-sided conversation certainly wouldn't hurt, and might even prove useful to the patient's recovery.

Jillian was hardly ever out of the room. Though her learning in communication had come to a standstill, she had been very eager to learn what she could from the doctor and the woman he sent in to do nursing care. She watched everything closely, and she had her stepmother explain as much as she could once the doctor had given Dianne instructions. But the picture books, and the signed phrases were put to one side as she sat mutely by the sickbed, watching and waiting for her father to wake up from "SICK".

Since the time of Dianne's talk with the minister, she had spent every available moment after school hours at the bedside with Jillian, and they had watched and waited. But unlike her step-daughter, Dianne did speak. Her words were not open and chatty like Peter's or the minister's, but the few words she did utter were genuine and heartfelt. Inside her breast burned an evergrowing flame of affection, though she could think of no proper way to express what she was feeling.

The school children's progress did not falter for a moment. Dianne had settled back into that routine easily, and if it hadn't been for the uncertainty at home, she would have been very content.

Mary-Ann Todd continued to help with the housework occasionally, but Dianne found that she needed the extra work to keep her worried mind occupied. As the paid nurse only came in once a day, there were other smaller tasks that had to be seen to, which Dianne left in the hands of his willing daughter while the classes were in progress. Jillian was eager to follow the instructions and Dianne went to the classroom confident that neither father nor daughter would go anywhere while she was busy.

It was four weeks to the day, from the time of the accident, that, as Dianne was conducting a spelling test for the class, she was startled by the school door being thrown open. Alarmed, she turned around and saw Jillian, breathless and with tears on her cheeks, waving frantically for Dianne to come.

Without stopping to explain, Dianne dropped her book on the desk and ran after the child, panic knotting her stomach.

The path back to the house seemed to be interminable as Dianne wished she could call out to Jillian and ask her what was wrong. But she knew that there were no answers that way as she rushed around the house, in through the back door and straight to the end bedroom.

It only took a moment for Dianne to see that nothing seemed different from when she'd visited the room earlier in the morning. Richard was still lying on his back, his eyes closed and his colour much the same as it had been.

"Whatever made you come for me in such a hurry?" Dianne wondered out loud, while moving close to the side of the bed to feel for Richard's pulse. But even before she could pick up his wrist she saw his eyes begin to move beneath the eyelids as if he was attempting to open them, and she heard a faint sound in his throat.

"Richard," she breathed, smoothing her hand across his forehead and pushing away his wayward fringe "Can you hear me? Are you all right?"

"Dianne!"

He had spoken her name, a muffled, low sound - but it was her name. He understood that she was there, and Dianne was ecstatic.

"I'm here, Richard," she said quickly, desperate to establish communication. "Can you hear me? Please get well, please! Jillian needs you so much!"

She stopped waited and watched closely for a response.

"Did you hear me, Richard?" she repeated, softly this time. "Jillian needs you to get well!"

It was slow and seemingly an effort, but eventually, Richard forced his eyes wide open, and Dianne could see that he was focussed upon her.

"And you?" he asked her in a weak, strained tone.

"I need you, too, Richard," she said quietly, almost shyly. "Please get well."

"Are you just saying it because I'm sick?" It was obviously taking a lot of energy for him to talk, but Dianne heard what he said, and understood what he meant. Her heart melted and fighting back tears, she reached for his hand, taking it and squeezing it affectionately.

"I more than need you, Richard," she confessed gently. "I believe in you, and I love you."

He closed his eyes again, and for a few moments Dianne thought he had slipped back into the coma.

"Please get well, Richard. Please." Wide eyed and afraid, she looked closely for some response, and was almost sure that he'd slipped back into unconsciousness again when his lips parted and he spoke.

"You're always nagging me, Dianne," he whispered huskily.

All of the pent up emotion - fear, anxiety, the repressed love - released at that moment, and she began to cry. She realised that he was back. Still dazed, and somewhat weakened, but he was back and in full possession of his mind.

"I was so afraid that I'd lost you and I had been so confused about us. About me loving you. I should have told you, but I didn't know how, Richard. I didn't know how." She wept openly, laying her head on his chest. "I was so afraid I'd never get the chance."

She could hear his heart thudding steadily against his chest, and was content to stay there feeling that an emotional bond was forming between them, something that had been struggling for months, but had never had the opportunity for expression. She closed her eyes and accepted his touch as he lifted his hand and let it rest on her hair.

"I'm not that easy to get rid of," he said slowly. "Dianne, will you marry me?"

She lifted her head, suddenly worried that he had perhaps lost his memory.

"We are already married," she spoke evenly.

"No!" he contradicted her. "I mean, again." He paused as if to regain energy, then went on. "Only this time we'll add to love and to cherish."

Dianne's face broke into a broad smile as she understood what he meant.

"Yes, Richard," she whispered over the lump in her throat. "Yes, I'll marry you, and I will love and cherish you too."

It was at that moment that Dianne remembered that Jillian was in the room, and that she had been standing back, anxiously watching her stepmother and waiting for her to tell her everything would be all right. Still holding Richard's hand, she signed with her other hand for Jillian to come close.

"I LOVE FATHER," she signed, and smiled at the child.

"I LOVE FATHER," Jillian signed in return. The young girl turned her attention to the man whom she had guarded so carefully for the last few weeks, and when she saw him smiling at her, she tentatively moved closer. Richard responded by reaching his hand toward her, and she understood. The father and daughter embraced, and Dianne felt an overwhelming sense of joy.

The small wedding party that gathered in the Reverend Andrews' office contrasted sharply with the one that had been there over a year before.

The bride and groom held each other's hands, and were more than comfortable looking into each other's eyes as they repeated the sacred vows. Special emphasis was placed on the promises that had been sadly lacking at the first ceremony, and Mrs. Andrews had to wait her turn to offer her congratulations, as the couple lingered over the traditional wedding kiss.

There was no need to sign any papers on this occasion, as the legality of the union was as sound as it had been when they were first declared man and wife. But there was a definite melding of spirits. Whereas before Dianne had agreed to the marriage as the only solution to a very difficult situation; where she had struggled to even like the man, let alone trust or love him, now she felt very different. The year she had spent living with Richard Schrouder, learning more about him and his daughter, seeing his strengths and vulnerabilities, had taught her that there was more to the man than he let people see. Having seen him completely vulnerable in that coma, Dianne knew that even while struggling with troubles of the past, Richard meant something to her, and she now was prepared to trust her whole self to him, giving herself to him in true marriage.

Richard was not insensible to what this trip to the church office meant. He recognised his own deficiencies and the bitterness that had influenced his most recent years. He knew that he had not made things easy for Dianne to love him, and yet he knew that she did. He also knew that he loved her, and he was prepared to let his guard down long enough for her to see who he really was.

But neither of them thought too deeply about the complexities of their relationship on this day. For a few short hours at least, they allowed themselves to be swept into the romance of a love newly awakened, and a developing passion.

As they walked back to the schoolhouse following the ceremony, they walked slowly together, his arm around her shoulder, her arm about his waist. The difference in their relationship from what it had been before was clearly evident. Reverend Andrews and his wife saw it, and the Todds saw it as they watched them coming along the street towards their home.

Even the chore of moving her things from the cluttered office into the double bedroom was now shared, and done with an anticipation that made Dianne smile at her husband, and he grinned at her in return.

But the thing that marked the biggest difference from the first wedding was the fact that eleven-year-old Jillian was always there, watching their interaction closely, absorbing the happiness of the occasion and learning what it was to experience joy in her family.

Chapter Twenty-One

Richard's physical condition continued to improve slowly, but Doctor Stewart had insisted that Dianne maintain the responsibility of the school.

"You are going to have to be patient, Richard," Doctor Stewart spoke firmly to him when he objected. "Head injuries can have lasting effects, and I don't want you racing back to the classroom, over-exerting yourself, and having you back in bed."

Richard was not really happy with the situation, and he allowed his frustration to show to some degree. While Dianne loved teaching, and loved the children, she felt Richard's displeasure, even understood his frustration, but there was really little she could do about it. The Doctor had been very firm on this issue and Dianne was too afraid of causing some permanent damage to yield to her husband's ill humour.

It had been several weeks of her continuing in this position before Doctor Stewart sought her out during a break at school.

"I'll go and tell Richard you are here," she said as she got up from behind her desk.

"I want to speak with you alone, if that's all right, Mrs. Schrouder," Doctor Stewart said quickly.

Dianne sat down quickly, fearing the worst.

"It's not a serious matter," he was quick to reassure her, "that is to say, Richard will be all right."

Dianne breathed a sigh of relief.

"However, I'm afraid that he is not going to be able to shoulder the same work load that he has in previous years."

"Why?" Dianne asked. "He's getting well, isn't he?"

"Oh, yes!" Doctor Stewart sounded quite positive. "His condition is definitely improving, however..." He paused a moment as if searching for the right words. "It's just that there are a number of side-effects that can persist as a result of a blow to the head. I fear that there are a couple of things that are going to interfere with Richard's ability to perform at his former level of competency."

Dianne listened carefully, and realised that she had already noticed one or two things that would not normally have been a problem, daily headaches that seemed to materialise after any period of concentration, for instance. And a number of times when he simply couldn't recall information that she herself knew he knew. She told the doctor about these symptoms.

"I cannot be certain that it will be permanant at this stage," the doctor continued. "It is quite probable that these symptoms will improve, even disappear altogether, but if we just ignore them, and put Richard under the same obligation of responsibility he held before, we are not only likely to aggravate the symptoms but also increase his frustration to a point that could be quite overwhelming. Both of you are going to have to face the fact that he will not be able to return to work as he did before. If he comes back he is going to need help."

"Have you told him about this?" Dianne asked, suddenly very concerned about his reaction to this information.

"I haven't said anything to him, in so many words," he confessed, "but I think he knows. He has asked me about it many times. He is anxious about being so slow when he does try to work."

"Does he know that it won't improve?"

"Not even I know that, my dear," the physician said. "It is as the good Reverend says, 'in God's hands'!"

"Will you tell him exactly what you've told me, please, Doctor Stewart." Dianne knew that her strong-minded, independent husband would not take kindly to the news that he would have to remain dependent on someone else, and she shied away from being the one to tell him.

"I'll tell him, Mrs. Schrouder, but you are the one who is going to have to convince him to give up the school!"

The doctor's words continued to echo in her mind, long after he'd left, right through until she'd finished the afternoon classes.

Richard must give up the school!

The concept seemed so utterly awful to her. It was not just the consideration that there were no jobs to be found in the current economic depression, but also the fact that the personality of Richard Schrouder seemed to be so intertwined with the Carlton Public School.

Although Dianne had not been there during the many years of hard work and improvement, she knew that even the most disapproving townspeople would acknowledge that the school's success was due to the mysterious schoolmaster. For him to have to give up all that he had worked to build would be almost like giving up his whole life. After all, the school had *been* his whole life for nearly twelve years.

The back door would slam shut, just when Dianne wanted to make a subtle entrance. Richard looked up from the book he'd been reading, and watched her enter.

Immediately, Dianne knew that Doctor Stewart had told him as she could see the disappointment in his eyes.

"I'm sorry, Richard," she said softly. "I know how much it means to you. I only wish there was something..."

"There's nothing to be done, Dianne," he snapped in a manner reminiscent of months ago. "My usefulness is ended, and I am no longer required."

Dianne recognised his old habit of hiding behind harsh words, and she determined to counter it. "Stop talking like that!" she said firmly. "You are still very capable, and this school will be reduced to a pitiful state without you!"

"Are you trying to let me down gently, Dianne? Do you think I'm really that stupid? You know as well as I do that these townsfolk have been waiting for any excuse to drum me out of town, and now they have it!"

"Richard!" Dianne crossed the room and knelt down next to him, looking directly into his eyes so that he could make no mistake about what she was saying. "If they had really wanted you out of town; if they'd ever had a real reason to dismiss you, they would have done it by now. I said I believed in you, and I meant it. You have made some mistakes in the past, but that doesn't mean that you haven't also done a lot of good. I know it, and I'm guessing most people know it even if they haven't been able to get along with you. Now is the time to find a positive solution to the problem, not crumble in defeat."

He couldn't escape the intensity of her gaze, and he didn't like using the harsh pretence of past times any more. He wanted to hope, if Dianne would help him. She saw a hope dawn in his eyes and continued.

"Didn't you say that if we could raise some funds, the government would sponsor the rest necessary to employ a second teacher?"

"Dianne." He sighed but his tone was softer. "Please, Dianne. I know you mean well, and I don't want to be hard on you, but it just seems as if you're trying to raise false hopes. You know that I haven't been able to raise any money at all, let alone enough to meet the government's requirements."

"But, Richard," Dianne persisted, "you were so tied up with the running of the school that you never had time to put any real effort into fund raising!"

"You're doing it again," he said. "You're trying to make excuses for my mistakes. You know what the facts are, Dianne. I cut myself off from the parents and townspeople so much so that I doubt one of them would be willing to support me with sponsorship."

"You doubt too much," Dianne said quickly, and held his gaze daring him to contradict her. Eventually she continued. "I want you to give me permission to start a parents' and friends' support committee!"

"A what?" He seemed genuinely confused.

"A committee, Richard. A team of people who will work together on all sorts of supporting schemes - maintenance working bees, parents' social evenings, and most of all, a fund-raising effort!"

At first, Dianne thought her husband would revert to his usual negative response, and merely push her idea aside as ridiculous, but his face softened, and so did his tone.

"You believe in too many high ideals, Dianne," he sighed eventually. "I really think I've done too much damage to expect any parent in this town to lift a finger to assist me!"

"They may not right at this moment," Dianne agreed, "but as soon as they get to know just how wonderful you really are, they will be lining up with offers of support!"

Richard couldn't maintain his pessimism any longer, and a smile flitted across his face.

"With your faith in success, I can almost believe you might be right!"

Dianne reached up and quickly kissed his cheek.

"You won't regret it, Richard. I know we can make the money we need, and with a second teacher, you can retain your position as the headmaster!"

Chapter Twenty-Two

Dianne chattered excitedly as she helped Mary-Ann set out china teacups and saucers on the sideboard. Jillian hovered nearby, watching and waiting for another job to be assigned to her. The child's willingness to help was plainly evident in the eagerness in her face.

During the time that Richard had been in a coma, Jillian had become very close to him. She had understood, perhaps for the first time in her life, what it was to love someone, and to watch them suffer. Since the time of his recovery, Jillian's attention to any task that might help her father was intense. She didn't want just to please him, she wanted to help him, almost as if she understood the emotional depression that often caused him distress. When she understood that this afternoon tea was a way to help her father, Jillian's attention was focussed in a way that those who observed her could see it.

"That little girl is devoted to her father," Mary-Ann commented as she watched the girl work. "I do believe she is determined to succeed, just because it's for him!"

"So am I," Dianne said quietly.

Mary-Ann shook her head, still struggling with the change of attitude she was reluctant to admit. She had so completely joined in the town's anger, mistrust and dislike of the schoolmaster, and now that Dianne, whom she'd come to love and respect, was showing a true love and commitment to the man, she was finding it all very difficult to come to terms with.

"There's someone here, Mrs. Todd," Dianne called. *Please Lord, let me be successful. Help them to like us and our plan.* She prayed as her hostess went to answer the front door. She couldn't help the anxiety she felt, knowing that Richard had, by his own action, allowed his reputation to be badly damaged. Now she had no course of action left but to pray that God would help these people to see the Richard she knew, forgive him for his past rudeness and be willing to adopt a new attitude in wanting to help him help the school.

Dianne smiled sweetly at the two ladies as Mary-Ann showed them into the lounge room. She invited them to sit down on one of the many chairs that had been arranged around the room. Dianne recognised both women as mothers of some of her own students, and greeted them openly, asking after their children in turn. After offering them a cup of tea, Dianne signalled Jillian to take a plate of savouries across to serve them. Jillian understood and readily obeyed, but the ladies were caught somewhat off guard.

"I say," the taller woman spoke up. "What's your name, girl?" She did not reach for one of the carefully prepared refreshements, as Jillian had expected she would do, and of course, Jillian did not hear her speak the question.

"What's the matter with you, child?" the woman demanded. "Answer me, when I speak to you!"

"Mrs. Shannon," Dianne saw the problem and tried to forestall it straightaway. "Jillian cannot hear you...."

"There's no need for you to be making excuses, Mrs. Schrouder," the offended guest snapped back at her. "I know where it is that the child gets her bad manners! This is that schoolmaster's daughter, I take it?"

"Now see here, Edith," It was Mary-Ann who intervened in a firm tone this time. Dianne flashed a glance across to see her come back into the room, with some new visitors, her hands on hips and a scowl on her face. "You have no call to come into my house and insult my friends..."

"It's all right, Mrs. Todd, please." Dianne attempted to diffuse the situation.

"No, Dianne," Mary-Ann objected. "This has gone on long enough. I think it is about time we all started acting like the Christian women we call ourselves!"

"Well, I never, Mary-Ann Todd," Edith Shannon was utterly offended now. "I must say you've come down a peg or two, in my eyes at least, when you take the part of an ill mannered child, and then turn on your own friend, hauling me over the coals for a simple correction in her behaviour. Don't tell me that schoolmaster has bewitched you, along with Mrs. Pierceson here!"

A burst of emotional chatter broke out amongst all the ladies present, and by the angry disapproving looks cast in Mary-Ann, Dianne and Jilllian's direction it was obvious just how bad public opinion really was.

"Please, Mrs. Todd," Dianne struggled to gain control of the situation, while trying to remain calm, and also trying to reassure one very frightened child. "Don't say anything else. I will apologise."

"As if you should!" Mary-Ann retorted.

But Dianne had already begun to face the excited group of ladies, and had cleared her throat ready to speak.

"Mrs. Shannon," she began once the noise began to die down. The ladies gradually stopped talking, and glared at Dianne, obviously waiting for an explanation. But there were no expressions of patience and understanding among them.

Only indignation and scepticism. "I must apologise, for my step-daughter's apparent rudeness...."

"As I said before, Mrs. Pierceson, it is no more than what I'd expect from a child of *his*!"

"I'm sorry you see it that way." Dianne chose to ignore the hurtful comment and pushed on. "I know that Jillian here, would dearly love to greet you, if only she could!"

It was as if they were all loaded and ready to fire the next barbed retort, but Dianne's statement disarmed them momentarily, and a stunned silence held for a few moments.

"So, she's a dim-wit then," another woman said nastily. "I guess there is no wonder then..."

"Lillian Steele!" Mary-Ann's patience had run out. "You are the only dim-wit present. Can't you see that the poor little mite is deaf, and has been since birth!"

"Deaf!" The one word was muttered by just about all who had joined the lively argument, and each woman's tone expressed their surprise and perhaps a small amount of chagrin.

"Yes!" Mary-Ann said smugly. "Deaf! And the poor child has been suffering for years without a mother, in a prison of silence."

"Well, what happened to her mother, I'd like to know?" the subdued Mrs. Steele seemed set to battle again. "I shouldn't wonder she ran off, with that impossible husband she had to endure!"

Dianne was hurt by the comment, but she took a deep breath and determined she would remain focussed on setting the record straight rather than courting more trouble by holding a grudge.

"Look, I'm sorry, Mrs. Pierceson," Lillian Steele went on, sounding anything but sorry. "I'm sorry that you have found yourself saddled with this antisocial tyrant..."

Dianne lifted her head in defiance, and glared angrily at
the outspoken woman. "My name is Mrs. Schrouder." Her
voice threatened to break under the strain of the emotion
behind it. " I am proud of that name because I am proud of
the husband who gave it to me. Oh, I know that he appears
hostile and mysterious on the outside, and there was a time
when even I thought unkind things about him, just as you
are doing now, but Richard Schrouder is not a monster,
neither is he a tyrant. He is a normal, loving father and
husband, who has been caught in a trap of loneliness and
despair for some years now. Don't think he doesn't know
what all of you think of him. He knows! He knows you're all
waiting for the opportunity to condemn him." She paused,
gathering her thoughts, and breathing deeply for courage.
"How do you think he felt when the baby he'd wanted so
much, was found to be deaf? How do you think he felt, when
the child's mother took desperately ill, and suddenly died. He
was alone, ladies. Alone and hurting with no-one to reach
out and care for him. Oh, he will admit, as readily as I, that
he has made mistakes. He admits it, and suffers under a cloud
of regret, knowing that there is little he can do to make up
for it — because he doubts that anyone would be willing to
give him a chance to say sorry, to live differently.

"You know, as well as I do, what a good teacher he is and
how much work he has done to improve our little school. And
yet, heartlessly and thoughtlessly, you are willing to condemn
him for that which is a result of tragic circumstances."

It had taken a lot of courage for Dianne to speak in the
face of such open hostility. She had struggled to keep her
voice from breaking, and had to blink hard to keep the tears
stinging her eyes from forming. Now that she had finished,
nobody in the room seemed to be able to speak. The silence
persisted for a few moments, and most eyes turned in

Mary-Ann Todd's direction, as if she as hostess would be the one who would say what to do next.

"Ladies." she eventually spoke. "My friends. I am ashamed to admit that as much as any of you, I have misjudged Richard Schrouder, and because of my prejudice and unfair speculations I shut out of my heart both him and his delightful daughter. I'd heard and repeated some terrible rumours about the man, and I'm ashamed to admit that they were only rumours. There was no truth in any of it. But my young friend, Dianne, saw past the outside appearances, took the risk to know Richard Schrouder and discovered the truth about him and his daughter, Jillian. I admit at first I thought she had lost her mind, but I can see that what she's saying is true. Richard Schrouder is essentially a good and upright young man. It's true that, like most of us he has his faults, but like the rest of us he is deserving of our respect and support, and even our love. Yes, love! We busily call ourselves Christians, and yet we have withheld from him the very thing that Christ himself has told us was so important."

"Well, that's all very well for you, Mary-Ann Todd," Mrs. Shannon found her voice again, "but how do you expect us to show love and respect to a man who isn't even willing to give a person the time of day?"

"Please, Mrs. Shannon," Dianne interceded. "I am fully aware my husband has been less than friendly and open in the past, but I'm also aware of the hurt and suspicion he's had in return. This animosity caused him to withdraw even more."

"It's all very well for you to excuse his behaviour, Mrs. Pierceson, I'm sorry, Mrs. Schrouder..."

"I'm not excusing his behaviour, Mrs. Shannon. I'm only relaying to you his regret and his apology, and a request for a chance to begin again."

Chatter broke out again amongst those gathered, each one insisting on adding her own thoughts about the situation.

"So what is it your husband proposes?" Lillian Steele asked, with a note of scepticism still in her voice.

"Actually, Mrs. Steele, my husband is proposing he resign gracefully, before he is forced to leave!"

"What!" Mary-Ann looked at her, horrified. "Then why all of this, if he just wants to leave?"

"I didn't say he wants to leave, Mrs. Todd. Nothing could be further from the truth!"

"What then?" another lady prompted.

"As you know," Dianne continued, "my husband has only just recently recovered from the effects of a rather nasty accident."

There was a general nod of affirmation and murmuring around the room.

"Unfortunately, he is still struggling with some of the effects of the injury. Generally, he copes with things very well, but when it comes to intense study or intricate hand work, he suffers from terrible headaches, and cannot seem to complete familiar tasks in twice the normal time, if at all. Doctor Stewart has recommended that he give up the school. It's simply too much work for him to handle alone!"

"Well, I guess I can admit that he has put in more than his fair share, where our children are concerned," a short, stocky woman commented. "I shall be sorry to see him have to leave." It seemed that most everyone in the room was prepared to agree with this comment.

"This is the reason why I have asked our hostess, Mrs. Todd, to call this gathering." Dianne finally began to talk about her plan. "Some time ago my husband applied to the education department to have a second teacher's position approved.

They accepted his application and gave permission, and that is how I came to live in your town, as your second teacher."

"And a fine job you did, too, Mrs. Pierceson," one of the younger mothers spoke up.

"Thank you, Mrs. Skene." Dianne acknowledged the comment. "However there was a condition on the position, and that was that my husband was to raise a certain amount of the wage from the Carlton public. Because he had withdrawn so much from the community, coupled with the intensive duties of caring for Jillian and the school, he was unable to raise any such money at all, and so he was forced to dismiss me from that position."

"More's the pity," someone mumbled.

"He was released to run the whole school more effectively once we married, and I was able to take charge of Jillian, but now, you see, it's impossible for him to manage as he did before the accident. I don't want him to give up the school that he has worked so hard for, or the children that he genuinely cares about. I'm proposing to you ladies that we begin a parents' and friends' committee for the school, a group of willing workers who can raise the funds necessary for the second teacher, and as a consequence see my husband retained as headmaster."

Dianne unconsciously held her breath as she watched all those gathered begin to discuss the matter. She had her arms around Jillian who had backed into her to find security during the earlier confrontation, and she gave her what she hoped was a reassuring smile. She had done everything within her power to rally support. Now, it was up to the willingness of these people to forgive, and their willingness to work for the benefit of a school under the direction of her husband.

Chapter Twenty-Three

Richard Schrouder looked up from the work he was doing at his desk when he heard Dianne and Jillian come in through the back door. The headache he'd been trying to ward off was evident as his brow furrowed in an attempt to cope with the pain.

"Headaches again?" Dianne saw the frown and showed her concern. Without waiting for him to answer she moved around behind his chair and began to massage his shoulders. He sat up straight in response to her touch.

"How did it go?" he asked, not really sure if he wanted to hear the answer.

"It went very well," she spoke close to his ear. "They are going to help us - to help you!"

He turned around to study her face, hardly daring to believe what he'd heard. Dianne saw his doubt and went on.

"The Parents' and Friends' Support Committee is officially up and running!" she said, smiling. "All the ladies were chattering about ideas of how they can raise the money you need. We've already planned a trading table, a luncheon, and a huge family fete. It won't be for several months but we have to start organising now. It's going to be the biggest event of all."

"They're really going to help you?" Richard asked still struggling to believe this could be true. "Are you sure they understand that it is to help me?"

"They know all about it Richard. It seems that they have accepted your apology, and have decided to give you another chance."

"Will it work, Dianne?" he asked, still unwilling to accept the good news. "Do you think that we can raise all that money?"

"We have to, my love, because if we don't, there is no way you can run this school alone. We have to have the second teacher, you must face that fact!"

"I have faced it," he said quickly, "but there is something you've forgotten, you know."

"What have I forgotten?" she asked, puzzled.

"You!" He looked at her hopefully. "With you as the second teacher, I know we could manage!"

"But isn't there something you've forgotten, Richard," Dianne contradicted. "Who is going to look after your children?"

Richard smiled at her as he stood up, reaching out to embrace her. "You will never know how grateful I am for what you have done for me. For Jillian and me. I never knew just how lost I was, and how lonely. I had my daughter here, but I never knew her, and didn't have any idea that she could love me. But you've helped us past all that, and now even I believe that Jillian is advanced enough to actually sit in class with you. You can really communicate with her, and she is learning so much. This could be really good for her."

"I think you are quite right, that being in class would be a very good step in Jillian's education, however," she paused and looked up at him, "There is your other child to consider."

Instantly Richard stiffened. It was not the response Dianne was expecting by any means.

"What are you saying, Dianne?" he said in a tentative tone.

"I'm trying to say that we are going to have a baby. I won't be able to teach for much longer."

She had said it straight out. He couldn't misunderstand what she was saying, but his response was hard. His features had lost the spark of hope and expectation, and he tore his gaze from hers. Stepping away from the embrace, he turned around and walked out of the room.

Dianne was crushed. It was the Richard she had first known. Distant, cold and probably, she guessed, retreating behind his security wall because there was something he couldn't face. But what was it he couldn't face? Dianne didn't have any idea. For a few moments she thought she might herself withdraw and harden her own heart to his harsh reaction, but she couldn't. It had been too long a fight to this point, just to let it go, so she pulled herself together and went to find him.

"Richard!" She spoke quietly once she'd entered their bedroom and found him sitting on the edge of the bed. "Are you all right?"

He didn't answer her but continued to stare unseeingly at the wall.

"Didn't you understand what I was trying to tell you?" she pursued gently.

"I understood, Dianne," he said. "You're expecting a baby – my baby!"

"Yes! Yes, Richard. I am! And I'm very happy about it. Aren't you?"

"How can I be?" The question was like a trigger and Richard spoke despairingly. "How can I be happy when I remember where it got me last time."

"I don't understand." Dianne faltered and her voice began to waver with emotion.

"Last time, when Helen told me she was having a baby, I was happy - I was deliriously happy!" He began in a low and even tone. "I told all my friends. I shocked my family by boasting out loud about it, and when we shifted here I let everybody know just how proud I was of my wife and the little baby she would soon have."

"I know, Richard," Dianne said quietly. "Mr. Todd has told me about it."

"But then, after the baby was born, and after I'd made a great fuss about how beautiful she was and how clever and responsive she was, then it happened!"

Dianne didn't prompt him. She knew he would tell her the whole story now.

"The baby was not progressing at the same rate as other children in the town. I started to scold Helen and told her to spend more time trying to teach Jillian little tricks. Helen tried, I know she did. I guess she wanted me to be happy with our baby, and with her, but my pride told me that, as the schoolmaster, my baby had to be brighter and more advanced than all the others, and my pride was being hurt. I guess I became unreasonable. I know I made ridiculous comments about neglect and carelessness. But at the time, all I could feel was my own disappointment and how I felt that it was the talk of the town. Eventually, Helen sought professional help for Jillian, and it was found that she was deaf. Helen was too scared to tell me. She had the doctor inform me that my baby would never hear or speak.

"I became swallowed up in self pity. All I could think of was how I felt, how I was disappointed and hurt. And I didn't stop for one moment to think how Helen must have been feeling, of how frightened and hurt she must have been by it all. All I could think was how she had borne me a child that was less than perfect. I felt as if I had to have someone to blame. I told her she couldn't have another child. I made her feel as if Jillian's deafness was her fault."

He sighed heavily as he saw, possibly for the first time, just how wrong he had been. Dianne didn't dare break into his thoughts so remained silent.

"Then she told me she was going away!" Richard continued. "She said that the doctors had ordered it, but I didn't believe her. I told myself that she was trying to run away from the mistake *she* had made. I didn't go with her, as a loving caring husband should. I only went to visit her once, and in my heart, I have to admit, it was only to make her come back and look after the child. I didn't know she was dying, Dianne. In all reality, she was already dead. I had killed every bit of life she had in her. Every spark of hope and love we'd ever shared. I did it. Me and my bitter pride, wanting to blame everyone but myself. She's dead, and I feel as if I killed her myself - not physically - but I killed her spirit.

"I can't help but think it's happening all over again. I loved her, Dianne, just like I love you, and I'm scared. What if I do the same to you as I did to her. What was wrong with me? I can't face it, just knowing she died without knowing I actually loved her; without her knowing that I know it was my fault and I'm sorry. I just can't face all that again!"

Dianne couldn't speak and she couldn't move. What Richard had told her was tragic. He knew what he had done was wrong, but there was no way now that he would ever be able to make it right. His first wife was dead and there wasn't any chance of saying he was sorry.

Richard lifted his eyes to hers and she knew he was searching for a response. She knew how easy it would be to turn away from him in disgust, to hold against him the terrible things he'd done. He knew it too, and the two stared at each other, held in the moment of deciding what should be done.

"I'm sorry, Richard." Dianne eventually managed to speak. "I'm sorry for Helen, I'm sorry for Jillian, but mostly I'm sorry for you."

There was a pause. There was nothing else that Richard could say. He was at her mercy.

"I forgive you, though it doesn't really matter about me. The question is, would Helen have forgiven you if you had asked her?"

She waited, watching as he seemed to search his heart for a response. The atmosphere was strained as she watched him slowly shake his head.

"I don't know!" he said sadly. "I wish I knew, but I don't!"

The torture of not knowing was real, and Dianne felt it. She was searching frantically through her own thoughts looking for a word or action that would make things better, but it was so hard. The situation so impossible.

"What about Jillian?" she eventually suggested. "Is she like her mother? I mean, I know it's said that she looks like her, but is she like her in nature also?"

Richard appeared to be thinking the question through as he paused before answering. Dianne continued to search his face for an answer.

"It's no use, Dianne," he finally blurted out in defeat. "Even if Jillian would forgive me, I still can't ever know - I mean really know. I hurt Helen so badly, Dianne. I was so cruel to her."

Dianne turned away in resignation. She wasn't about to deny the seriousness of the charge. She knew that Richard had been terrible to his first wife. But she did want to see him break through the guilt and pain of the past. But wanting something wasn't going to be enough in this instance. The guilt seemed just to hang there like a black cloud over their lives. And with this frustration came the knowledge that her own precious news would have to be put aside. She was going to have a baby. Even her marriage to Samuel had not provided her with this joy, and yet now, just as her heart's desire of having a child was answered, there was a dark cloud over it all.

Leaving Richard in the bedroom, she went about her own business, but her thoughts were full of ideas of how she could prove to her husband that his first wife would have forgiven him. There were many possibilities, but no guaranties. Nevertheless, Dianne determined she would find the answer, if not for Richard, then for their baby.

Chapter Twenty-Four

Though Dianne wanted to share the news and the joy of her first child with everyone, she told no-one. She had no answers for the guilt that Richard was living under, and she didn't want to upset the delicate balance they had achieved by deliberately provoking a raw issue. She felt as if her hands were tied and so she chose the best course of action - to pray for her husband.

Richard went about his normal routine quietly, but Dianne felt that his spirits were low. She worried about his dejection, but she already knew there was nothing she could do to change it, so she smiled at him and went about her busy schedule. In some ways it was good that there was more than usual that required her attention, as this kept her focus from the difficulties. There was planning for the fete, helping with the school, and of course, maintaining the house.

But even though the extra activity engaged her mind and helped her avoid worry, it soon began to take its toll on her physical well being. Nearly every night she was exhausted long before normal bed time.

Mary-Ann had been watching the young couple closely, and noted the deterioration in Dianne's health. She applauded her commitment to the tasks at hand and admired her work ethic, but she couldn't help but be concerned by what she saw.

"I don't know what's wrong with Dianne." She brought the subject up with her husband one afternoon. "Something's not quite right and I think you should talk to Richard about it, see if there's something we can do to ease her work load."

"Do you think she's working too hard?" Peter hadn't seen what his wife had, and was taken aback.

"Well, I don't know, but I do know that she is not a hundred percent and shouldn't be working at the pace she's been keeping up these last few weeks. Something's wrong, and I think you should see what it is."

"I hardly think it's our business…" Peter began.

"Helen wasn't our business either, was she, and we stayed well out of it where she was concerned, and look how that turned out!" Mary-Ann was not going to be moved.

Peter couldn't disagree with this argument, and eventually prepared himself to visit his neighbour across the road.

"Dianne's certainly enthusiastic about this fundraising effort," Peter commented after they'd greeted each other.

Richard gave an unconvincing nod of his head, a weak gesture that Peter couldn't fail to notice.

"I hope you're all keeping well," Peter probed further.

Once again, Richard's response was neither detailed nor convincing. Peter waited momentarily, watching to see if Richard would take up the direction of the conversation, and in truth hoping he would give some clue as to whether Mary-Ann's worries had any foundation to them. But Richard remained vague and unwilling to pursue any conversation.

"I can't help but notice," Peter eventually went on, "and please forgive me for saying so, but it would appear things are not altogether what they should be with you."

"What do you mean?" Richard was instantly defensive.

"Settle down, son," the older man soothed. "I don't mean to pry, but it would appear that something is weighing on your mind."

"Even if there is, it's none of your business." Richard was unnecessarily rude in making this answer.

But Peter had learned a thing or two in the past months, and he wasn't going to be put off by rudeness. He pushed his chin out defiantly, and looked his neighbour squarely in the eye. "I've minded my own business for a long time, sir, and have left you to yours. But I was wrong. You've been struggling for years over here on your own, lonely and angry, with no-one to show any care or support. I'm not about to be turned around by your rude behaviour now. We can see something is wrong, and I mean to find out what it is. I cared about Helen, but I left it too late to help her. I'll be blowed if I'll make the same mistake again!"

Peter's words snapped Richard out of his state of self-pity. The mention of it being too late for Helen struck his conscience heavily. He knew Peter wasn't trying to pry more than he was trying to help him, and he had to make a deliberate decision to push aside his habitual reserve. He had no desire to push away the one man who really did understand and care.

"I'm sorry, Peter," he finally sighed. "You're right. Things aren't well. Not well at all, I'm afraid."

"What is it?" Peter spoke encouragingly.

Richard didn't answer straight away, but retreated into his thoughts. Peter waited patiently for a few moments before speaking again.

"Aren't you happy with the way Dianne is arranging things?" he asked.

"It's not that, Peter." Richard shook his head. "I can't even really figure it out for myself, let alone explain it to you.

"It doesn't matter how it sounds," Peter encouraged. "Say what you're thinking, and we'll try and sort the truth out from that."

"I didn't want to fall in love with her," Richard eventually blurted out. "Not after what happened last time." He paused for a moment. "But I did, and now it's happening all over again. I'm going down the same path I did with Helen."

"What path?" his friend pursued. "What's happening again?"

"Dianne's having a baby, Peter," Richard confessed, "and it's tearing me up!"

"How? How can your wife's having a baby tear you up?"

"She wants me to be happy, but I can't. All I can feel is panic and fear. I shouldn't have let myself love her in the first place!"

"I don't understand your logic, son," Peter said, bewildered.

"Don't you see, Peter? What happened when Jillian was born destroyed Helen and me. We'd been happy before that, and then it all fell apart. And now it's happening all over again!"

"Now just a minute, Richard!" Peter held up his hand. "What happened between you and Helen was not the baby's fault. You were both to blame to some degree, but not Jillian. She didn't choose for her father to get all pumped up with pride and to start being cruel to her mother. She didn't make you become bitter and hard. Those things entered your life by your own choice, and your choice alone! You have no right to be blaming the child for what happened then, and no right to be assuming this child will make it happen again! None of those dreadful destructive things can affect your relationship or your life unless you allow it to!"

Richard turned away from his friend, blinking back the tears that stung his eyes.

"Dianne deserves better, Richard," Peter went on. "Oh, yes! Helen deserved better too, but it's too late for her." He paused to let this idea take effect. "But it's not too late for Dianne, is it? The only things that can destroy you, Richard Schrouder, are your own bad attitudes and choices. If I were you I'd be pulling myself together and doing the very best I could for my wife!"

There was silence between the two men for what seemed like a long time, and Peter suddenly wondered if perhaps he had gone too far. But eventually Richard turned back towards him.

"I want to be happy, Peter. I want to love Dianne and the baby, but I have to admit I'm afraid. Afraid of myself and what I might do to them both. Deep down I always knew it was me who was to blame where Helen was concerned, but I was too proud to admit it, and now, as I do openly acknowledge my fault, I can't help but wonder if I'll do the same again!"

"Why should you?" Peter said. "Why should you think you might do it again? You love Dianne, don't you?"

"Of course I do, but I loved Helen as well, and that didn't stop me!"

"Come on now, son." Peter spoke coaxingly. "You have got to forgive yourself for the past. God forgives you, but it won't do you a scrap of good if you don't forgive yourself!"

"If only I could ask Helen to forgive me," Richard admitted his burden. "It would be all right then. But not knowing, Peter, that's what makes it impossible to forgive myself!"

"Have it your own way, Richard," Peter stated finally. "I can't force you to see sense, and let go of this all consuming guilt. But whatever you do, give Dianne some of the happiness *she* deserves!"

Chapter Twenty-Five

The smell of roasting meat wafted from the kitchen to tantalise Richard's senses as he approached the back door to his house. His appetite was immediately stirred by the tempting aroma, but it wasn't enough to shake the depression that had been settled in his soul for what seemed like forever.

Peter Todd's strong words still rang in his mind, and he struggled inwardly, tossing back and forth whether he could simply let go the guilt, as well as all the rest of the burden.

If only it were that simple, he thought to himself, failing to master the wave of negative thinking that had been his constant companion for many years. But then Peter's advice came back into his thoughts. *I can't keep thinking like this.* Richard physically shook himself as if to help break the mental pattern. *I'm going to completely destroy my whole family. Peter's right! I have to overcome this somehow. I have to, for Dianne's sake.*

Having steeled himself once again, Richard decided that he would act positively right away, before self-doubt came to knock him down again.

"Dianne!" He called out as he approached the kitchen, but was disappointed to find that it wasn't his wife moving about preparing tea, but his daughter. Despite this frustration, he smiled at the child, and saw again the likeness of his first wife smiling back at him.

"WHERE'S MOTHER?" he signed to her.

Jillian put down the vegetable she had been peeling so that she could reply. "MOTHER - SLEEPING" she signed. "WORK - TOO MUCH"

Jillian's simple observation pierced his heart deeply. He was hit with the full realisation that as the husband he had not been taking proper care of his wife. He moved quickly before regret chased him back to his own well of self-pity. She wasn't hard to find, curled up and fast asleep on the lounge room couch. Quietly, he stood and watched her sleeping for a few minutes. So many feelings arose in his chest, regret being one of the strongest. *God help me!* He prayed. *Help me to see past myself. Please don't let me do to her what I did to Helen.*

Kneeling down beside the couch, he reached out his large hand, and placed it on Dianne's swelling abdomen, waking her as he did so.

"What is it, Richard?" she asked groggily, woken suddenly by his unexpected touch.

"The baby's growing, isn't it?" He kept his gaze away from her face, almost too ashamed to see what response would be there.

"Yes!" Her answer was calm, almost calculated. "It won't be many more weeks before the whole town will know! I won't be able to keep it a secret for much longer!"

Richard couldn't form any sensible words over the emotion that had tightened his throat, but he could see that she was waiting for some sign of acknowledgment.

"I'm sorry!" He managed to say, but it was hard, as he felt that he was near tears. "Will you forgive me, Dianne," he continued with effort. "I know I've treated you so badly! Can you ever forgive me?"

Dianne quickly sat up, though it was a struggle. She reached out her hand and touched his cheek. "Of course I forgive you," she paused just a brief moment. "I love you, Richard! All I want is for you to be happy. I'm only sorry that you don't want the baby!"

"I do want the baby, Dianne. I just let negative things get the better of me sometimes, and I've acted like a fool, but I love you, you and the child, and I want you to be happy too!" He felt more confident to meet her gaze and was reassured by the sincerity he saw in her eyes. "Peter has given me a good talking to. I'm sorry Dianne, sorry that it came to that point that I needed such a jolt. I'm really sorry that what happened between Helen and me is forever coming between us. I wish there was some way to resolve it permanently."

"Dearest Richard," she whispered in his ear. "It can be resolved. It's within your grasp. All you need to do is take hold of it!"

"Please, Dianne..." he turned from her, pained by what he thought were simplistic promises.

"Listen to me!" She grabbed his shoulders and forced him to look back in her direction. "For better or for worse, I have made contact with your father-in-law...."

"How could you?" His eyes flashed with the old anger and painful memories.

"I could, and I did, Richard." Dianne was not going to be intimidated now. She'd come too far. "He's Jillian's grandfather, at the very least, and has a right to hear of her well-being!"

Richard stuck his chin out stubbornly as she continued to tell him what she'd done.

"Whether you want to face the fact or not, Richard, Helen's father is the only person who may hold the key to your guilty feelings. If you will just speak to him, you might finally be able to set your mind at rest!"

"His forgiveness is not the same as Helen's!" Richard's words showed that he was at least considering the possibilities.

"But he was with her to the last, Richard. He would know how she felt. There must be something to be learned from speaking with him."

"Maybe," he conceded reluctantly. "But I doubt he would condescend to see me after what I did to his daughter."

Dianne put her arms around his neck, and rested her forehead against his. "He will see you, my dear man. He is only waiting for me to get back to him with a suitable time!"

Dianne moved about the house happily, her energy levels boosted considerably by the anticipation she felt. She'd written the letter to Jillian's grandfather and invited him to come. She'd made arrangements with the Todds for him to stay at their place, just in case of any awkwardness. But she had high hopes that this visit would bring about something good. She didn't know what, but she was more hopeful of a positive outcome than she had ever been since becoming mistress of the school house.

Today was the day. Mary-Ann Todd had already been over once. Mary-Ann had become a regular visitor of late, the two women chatting over tea and scones, knitting and sewing in preparation for the new baby. But today, Mary-Ann had been to give Dianne some extra help to do a thorough clean of the school house. Dianne was so determined to have everything just so for when James Harnen arrived, that Mary-Ann was afraid she would wear herself out.

But far from being worn out, Dianne was energised by the prospect of the afternoon's meeting. She knew it was not necessarily going to be easy for either man, but she was

so optimistic about the outcome, so hopeful that Richard
would find release from the guilt that constantly ate at him,
that she found herself repolishing pieces of furniture that
already shone brightly.

Jillian had sensed the excitement in the air and had asked
her step-mother about it. Dianne took great pains to try
and instil the concept of grandfather - her mother's father
- into the child's understanding, but she was doubtful that
Jillian had fully understood what she had been trying to
convey.

Whether she understood the importance of what was
going on or not, Jillian hovered about her much-loved stepmother, carefully observing, patiently waiting for any signal
that might indicate her help might be needed. They arranged
and re-arranged the furniture, turned out several batches of
baking from the oven, set the table and arranged flowers.

It was into this hive of activity that Richard walked,
returning from his Saturday morning chores of cutting
wood for the school fires, and cleaning the classroom.

"Dianne," he spoke firmly, "you are working too hard. I
don't want you wearing yourself out, no matter who's
coming!"

"It's important. This is the first time Jillian will have met
her grandfather, and I want it to be a memorable occasion
for both of them!"

Richard sighed at the reminder. "I hope this works out
how you want, Dianne, because it is going to be terribly
hard on you if it doesn't!"

"Oh, shush!" she scolded. "Please don't talk like that, not
today, Richard. This is one of the most important days of
our life together. Please try to look on the bright side."

She turned back to her work, determined to ignore the
possibility of failure.

As the appointed hour for James' visit drew near, Dianne finally sat down, just as Richard had predicted, totally worn out.

Richard entered the lounge room dressed and ready to greet his former father-in-law and he instantly saw that his wife was exhausted. He began to tell her he'd told her so, and ordered her to go and lie down.

In her heart, Dianne wanted to protest and wave aside his concern, but her head was already spinning with tiredness and she could not deny that she desperately needed a rest.

"Come on, you silly child!" He spoke good-naturedly as he helped her up from the chair. "Go and rest for a while, and come to greet the visitors when you feel better!"

"I'm so sorry, Richard. I wanted everything to be perfect."

"I'll explain to them. They'll understand, I'm sure!"

Dianne gratefully went to her bed, relieved that her husband was being so supportive.

Richard spent some time with Jillian, carefully communicating his wish that she stay in her room until he called for her. He felt that to introduce her first off would take away the time he and his father-in-law needed to sort through the hurts and misunderstandings of the past.

The ticking of the mantle clock seemed to echo loudly around the room as Richard stood by himself waiting, straining his ears to hear the sound of approaching footsteps. The quietness seemed to accentuate the anxiety that had been building over the past weeks of waiting. By the time the knock came at the door Richard found he had broken out in a cold sweat, with all the doubts and regrets converging to assail him.

He quickly rubbed his clammy palms together in an attempt to present well, and made his way to the front entrance. Each step he took he tried to calm his racing heart.

Once he opened the door, Richard seemed like one caught in the glare of headlights, staring at the lined face of James Harnen. Eventually, Peter interrupted the difficult moment. "May we come in," he asked.

"Yes, come in," Richard answered lamely, called back to reality. "Dianne is not feeling well. I've sent her to rest!" All of his well-rehearsed speech had completely flown from his mind the moment he'd come face to face with Helen's father, for the first time in almost eight years. The moment he'd set eyes on him, all he could think of was: here was the man who was as dear to his late wife as he himself had once been.

"How are you, Richard?" the elderly, grey-haired man spoke simply.

Peter and Mary-Ann Todd stood back trying not to intrude on this reunion.

"James Harnen!" Richard addressed his father-in-law. "It's been such a long time!"

"Too long, son," he replied. "Far too long!"

A heavy silence descended upon the group as each one struggled to find the right thing to say. What seemed like a myriad of thoughts, some positive and some negative, ran through Richard's mind. He wanted desperately to ask about his late wife, and her final days, and yet he felt as if he should throw himself at her father's feet and beg forgiveness. As it was, no word or action materialised at all.

"I think I'll make some tea," Mary-Ann broke the uncomfortable silence.

"I'll give you a hand!" Peter used the excuse to leave the two principal characters alone. As the Todds left the room, the silence remained, but the anticipation rose to an almost unbearable level.

"I don't know what to say." Richard's voice was unstable and wavering as he eventually forced himself to speak. "So many hurts, so many wrongs. I just don't know where to begin!"

"I know, Richard." James Harnen glanced away at the wall, unable to look at his son-in-law's face. "I know I should have come sooner, but the longer I left it, the harder it became for me to admit the truth."

The expression on Richard's face showed that he didn't understand what James was trying to say. "What do you mean, James?" he asked. "The truth is, I mistreated your daughter and she died alone, believing she was unloved!"

For a moment Richard thought he saw James look even older than his years, his shoulders sagging further under the weight of a burden, as yet unrealised.

"That is the truth," Richard said again, "and it has been a matter of deep torment to me, knowing that there is now no way to make amends."

"I know that, son," James sighed heavily. "But sadly, that's not the whole truth!"

The younger man breathed deeply and pulled himself upright, as if the physical action could mirror his state of heart. "What is the whole truth, sir?" he asked, almost afraid to hear what the answer might be.

"I have done you great wrong, Richard," he sighed again. "I have been the cause of some of the greatest unhappiness I trust you will ever have to suffer!"

"What are you saying?" Richard began to tense, realising suddenly that there might be more to the painful past than he knew or understood.

"Helen asked to see you, Richard – often! Her aunt and I always told her that you had expressed a wish not to see her."

"What!" An almost unbearable pain gripped Richard's heart as he understood the implications of what he'd just been told. "You don't mean…"

"Personally, I didn't agree with my sister," James hurried on, "But I'm ashamed to admit I am spineless when it comes to standing up to her, and so I allowed her to dictate the terms, both to myself and to the hospital staff. She was determined to see you pay for your harshness to Helen. She had no sympathy for the way you'd made her life miserable, and she felt that it was your just desserts to be 'lumbered', as she put it, with the handicapped child!"

The waves of pain and regret continued to roll, at one moment self-blame, and then sheer frustration at knowing that Helen's aunt had deliberately tried to inflict more hurt when resolution might have been possible.

"I don't want to excuse myself from blame, son," James continued, "but I never did hold with my sister's bitter logic."

"I don't understand, James…" Richard eventually stuttered. "Do you mean to say that Helen…that Helen…"

"Helen told us all about you and the child. She came to us, in the city, in a terrible state. The truth is she couldn't cope with the child any more. At first, running away seemed like the only answer for her to escape your cruel insinuations. She knew she could never make the child into what you wanted, and so when the doctor prescribed the special care, it seemed like the perfect opportunity to get away from an impossible situation."

Richard put his hand up to his face and rubbed his forehead, sighing heavily as he did so. The weight of knowing he'd been the cause of her unbearable unhappiness settled heavily in his heart, like a rock.

"But she hadn't been in the hospital two days," James continued unwaveringly, "before she was crying and pleading with her aunt to send for the both of you. If she hadn't been so ill she would have gone straight home, but as it was, she remained, and because of what we'd told her, daily believing that you had refused to come."

"But I never received any such request." The new hurt was evident in Richard's tone. "I didn't even know she was dying!"

"I know, son," James replied, his tone heavy with regret. "I also know that when you finally did come of your own accord, my sister gave instructions to send you away. She was determined to see you pay!"

"I did love her, James. You've got to believe that!" He sounded desperate. "Oh, I know that I acted dreadfully and hurt her terribly over the matter of the baby, but inside, I knew I was wrong, and I wanted very much to make up. But my thinking got all mixed up with my stupid pride, and it stopped me from going to her before it was too late." He sat down, racked with the burden and regret.

"I'm afraid that I must take as much of the blame as yourself, Richard." James' voice wavered with emotion as he continued. "Near the end she called for you constantly, and yet I didn't have the courage to go against my sister's wishes, and even when Helen left you a letter, I withheld it from you."

"A letter?" The grieving young man lifted his head, tears glistening in his eyes. "She left me a letter?"

James nodded, tears in his own eyes, and he held out an envelope in his trembling hand. "I'm so sorry, Richard," he said, fighting a lump of emotion in his throat.

"A letter?" Richard said again in a hoarse whisper as he took it from his father-in-law's hand.

"I should have given it to you the day she wrote it, son. I should have come for you. There are so many things I should have done, but didn't. I have been burdened with the guilt of it all these years, and though I'm not deserving of it, I beg you to forgive me. Richard, I need to be free of this terrible feeling, knowing that I've let my little girl down. By hurting you, I've hurt her." His voice broke with emotion. "But even that doesn't seem as important as knowing that you had no other way of finding out, apart from myself, and I deliberately withheld that precious information from you."

Richard seemed not to hear the older man's plea as he turned the envelope over and over in his hands, still muttering incoherent words about 'a letter'.

Dear Lord, give me strength to face the truth, he prayed to himself. A strange stillness stole over the room as the two men focused their attention on the unopened envelope, which would at last satisfy the unanswered questions.

Richard slowly took his pen from inside his jacket, placed it in the opening, and methodically sliced through the aged seal.

"Dearest Richard," he began to read aloud, in a tone strained with emotion. *"I want so badly to see you, and yet I know that it is too late, for I feel myself fast slipping away. There is no more for me to do, but to ask your forgiveness. I have let you down terribly, and I wish, above all else, that I could make it up to you. There is no time now, and I cling desperately to the knowledge that you will forgive me. I know your good heart, Richard, and I regret that I will never hear your voice again, or feel your arms around me. Perhaps, one day, in the life that is to come, we will meet - without regret and without bitterness.*

Look after Jillian for me. Love her, Richard - please - love her for me.

I love you! I always have.

Helen.

As the last word on the page was read, the only sound left in the room was that of two grown men weeping.

Chapter Twenty-Six

Dianne had woken from her afternoon nap, and came down to the lounge room. Still shaking off some of the daze from waking, she came into the room to see Richard kneeling next to the worn armchair that contained both his father-in-law and his daughter, who was neatly perched on the old man's knee. She paused in the doorway for some time, watching the three of them. Even though only one was a stranger, she could not help but think that the other two, her husband and step-daughter, also looked strangely unfamiliar.

She had never noticed Richard's eyes as anything special before, but now, as she quietly observed him, she noticed a life dancing in those dark, brown depths that seemed to light his face with an expression of subdued joy. It took Dianne a few moments to process the change, but when she did, she suddenly realised that she had never seen just how handsome her husband was, for he had always worn a mask of hardness, probably in his attempt to hide the pain and guilt. She knew what must have happened. Somehow or other James had said what was necessary to release Richard from the burden he had been carrying ever since she'd known him. She smiled. She really liked what she saw.

She continued to observe the scene quietly, until she became aware of just how much she didn't belong to it.

Simply put, this was a family reunion in which she did not
'have a part. She hoped to slip away quietly to let the others
have some privacy to enjoy their reconciliation, but as she
moved, Jillian caught sight of her out of the corner of her
eye, and immediately she motioned for her step-mother to
come to them.

"Dianne!" Richard scrambled to his feet, a captivating smile
spread broadly across his face. Dianne couldn't believe the twist
of emotion in her stomach as she saw him like this. He was so
attractive she just wanted to throw her arms around his neck
and kiss him, but she restrained herself for propriety's sake.

"Come and meet Jillian's grandfather." Richard said,
oblivious to the effect he was having on his wife. "James
Harnen, this is my wife, Dianne."

The elderly gentleman got to his feet, Jillian having
removed herself the moment she saw Dianne, and he held
out his hand to take hers in a warm handshake. "I'm so
happy to meet you," James said with genuine feeling.

Dianne could not prevent the blood from rushing to her
face. She had not considered how difficult it would be for
her to come face to face with Jillian's grandfather, the man
who actually connected Jillian with her real mother. Just for
an instant, she felt like running away, as if she didn't really
belong here, but the warmth of James' greeting, and the
dramatic change in her husband soon chased away those
feelings of insecurity.

"I'm very pleased to meet you, sir," Dianne eventually
returned his greeting.

"Dianne." His voice was low and there was obviously a
tension in his throat. "I can never repay the debt I owe you."

"Please, Mr. Harnen..." she tried to brush away the
intensity of his gratitude.

"No, my dear," he hurried on, silencing her objections.

"You have given me a chance to renew my life. If it hadn't been for your unselfishness – for who could have blamed you if you'd wanted to keep Richard and Jillian to yourself? But you overlooked your own needs and gave me the opportunity to set right all the things that have been a source of misery for years."

Dianne looked confused for an instant, and a little embarrassed by his open expression of gratitude. She had thought that all the misery was on Richard's side, but now it was becoming apparent that James' visit had benefited both. She didn't quite know what to make of the situation for herself.

"He's right, Dianne," Richard said, as he caught her gaze with his own. "Perhaps you don't know quite how much you have done for both of us, but let me tell you, I feel as if I've just been set free from a prison."

"And I." James nodded as he spoke. "You have let God use you to help us, and I want you to know just how grateful I am."

Dianne stared at Richard, blinking her eyes in stunned amazement.

He leaned closer to her and spoke in a whisper for her ears alone. "I love you Dianne."

That was the clinching point. She had not known exactly when her feelings had turned toward Richard Schrouder. She could not mark a day on the calendar where she could say, 'on this day, I began to care for him'. But at this point, on this day, at this time, she realised how deeply she loved him. There was no more comparison between him and Samuel. Richard had found his own place in her heart, and she knew that, with this new release from the guilt of the past, she had found a permanent, cherished place in his.

For just a few moments, Dianne and Richard were lost in each other, the rest of the world had ceased to exist, but they were soon jolted back to the present by a small tugging on Dianne's skirt.

"Jillian," she whispered as she knelt down to her level and began to sign. "DO YOU LIKE GRANDFATHER?"

Jillian nodded enthusiastically, turning to the man in question and taking his hand.

"She likes you," Dianne said to him. "I wonder if she really understands who you are?"

"I was just going to show her this." As James spoke he held out a flat card to show them. "It is the only picture I have of her!"

Dianne took the old photograph and stared intently at it. In different shades of brown were the images of two people. She recognised Richard. He looked younger, almost like a boy dressed in his wedding suit, his hands placed on the back of an elaborate chair, upon which sat a young woman. His bride wore a simple wedding gown, with a crown of flowers and lace. But it wasn't her dress that caught Dianne's attention. It was her face, also childlike, but bearing a strong resemblance to the deaf child who now studied the old photograph.

"MOTHER," Dianne signed as she pointed to the image of the young bride.

Jillian looked up at her, confusion in her face. She glanced at the photo again, and Dianne could see that the child recognised her father as she pointed to his image and then to the man himself.

"MOTHER." Dianne pointed again to Helen's photograph and signed the term.

Jillian shook her head in response and pointed to Dianne, giving the familiar sign that meant 'mother'. She could not understand the stranger in the photograph.

Dianne stood up with a little assistance from her husband, took Jillian by the hand and led her out of the lounge, through the back porch, and outside to a place under the apricot tree.

"Where are they going?" James asked Richard as they watched them leave.

"I've stopped trying to understand how they communicate and learn, but they do."

Once under the shady tree, laden with ripening fruit, Dianne knelt down once again, signalling for Jillian to join her. Some weeks earlier, Dianne had found an injured sparrow in the garden. She had encouraged Jillian to nurse the ailing creature, hoping to instil a certain sense of responsibility, but sadly the tiny bird had died. Dianne had spent a long time explaining the concept of death to the child, although without the use of words it was a difficult task.

Now, as she knelt next to the tiny cross that marked the sparrow's grave, Dianne began to relate its death to the death of the woman in the photograph.

"FATHER LOVES MOTHER," she signed as she pointed to the two characters, "BUT MOTHER DEAD. GRANDFATHER BURIED MOTHER, LIKE WE BURIED SPARROW. GRANDFATHER AND FATHER SAD WHEN MOTHER DEAD."

Large tears began to form in Jillian's eyes as she began to comprehend Dianne's message.

"MOTHER LOVED JILLIAN. MOTHER LIVES WITH JESUS. NOW I'M MOTHER FOR YOU!"

The tears rolled down the child's face as she got up, turned and ran back inside. Dianne followed her, more slowly, and came back to the lounge room just in time to see Jillian signing to her father.

"SORRY - MOTHER - DEAD" she signed. "SORRY - YOU - SAD - AND GRANDFATHER - SAD"

Richard enfolded his daughter in his arms and allowed his own tears to mingle with those of his child, together finally expressing the grief for their loved one - a grief that had remained unexpressed since the time of her death.

Chapter Twenty-Seven

The old mattress had been dragged out of the shed again, given a thorough beating and airing, and put back into Richard's small office. James Harnen had scarcely hoped for acceptance of his apology, let alone the invitation to stay on in his son-in-law's home. He accepted, failing to hide his eagerness for wanting to get to know his young grand-daughter. There had been so many years wasted, and he was keen to make up for lost time.

Jillian responded in a delightful fashion to the presence of her grandfather. The two of them spent long hours together, each one learning about how to communicate with the other, and both determined to express their love.

Dianne was thrilled with the success. Not only had these two become re-united, but her husband was a different man also. She had never known him to be in such a state of happiness. Sometimes she was worried that it would not last, but the small mishaps and worries that would have upset him before, didn't seem to bother him any more. He seemed possessed of a new lease on life. There were moments when he seemed almost optimistic, and while this never failed to surprise Dianne, it thrilled her more.

But there were times when she didn't quite know how to take his overt affection. She had lived with him for so long without relying upon it, that now, as he spoke unfamiliar words of endearment and spent more time than she felt was necessary holding her in a loving embrace, she actually felt embarrassed by it.

"Richard," she scolded him one day. "You are behaving like a love-sick school boy!"

He smiled at her, not releasing his hold even slightly. "I don't care!" he replied flippantly. "When I should have been crazy about you, I wasn't, and so I want to make up for it now!"

Dianne laughed out loud at his logic, and pushed him into a nearby chair. "Well, you will have to control yourself, my love-sick baby, because I don't have the time or the energy to spend, with the fete so close at hand. There is still so much to do!"

He made a pout, pretending that he was hurt. But she could see through it.

"Come on, Richard," she laughingly pleaded. "You could give me a hand, you know."

"For you, I would do anything, my love!" He spoke in over-dramatised, romantic tones.

"Good!" she turned quickly to a note pad, tore off the top sheet and handed it to him. "You can see to this small list of jobs that need to be done before next Saturday!"

After a few moments of feigned objection, Richard left the room to begin the list of chores. Dianne sighed as she reflected on the current situation. Never, in all the time she had been at Carlton, did she imagine she could be so happy. A brief memory of Samuel crossed her mind, but this time she did not dwell on it. Somehow, the glory of the past had paled into insignificance, with the joy of the present outshining it.

★　★　★　★

As the day of the fete dawned, Dianne was up earlier than usual, her body full of nervous energy. She knew it was the anxiety of how the day would turn out that fuelled her, as her energy levels had been sadly lacking during the last few months of her pregnancy up until today.

Richard rose with her, aware that today marked the point of decision as to whether he would remain on as the head of the school or not. He knew his wife had organised and worked tirelessly on the fete, and he knew also that its success, if it did succeed, would be due solely to her determination.

"Honey." He took hold of her arm to prevent her leaving the bedroom. She stopped and searched his face. "I've been praying that today will be a success for you!"

"No, Richard," she corrected. "Today *will* be a success, but it will be for you."

He pulled her close and kissed her passionately, expressing his love and gratitude. "I don't know where I'd be without you," he whispered in her ear.

"Nor I, without you," she returned, just as sincerely.

Dianne looked up from her job of straightening a table cloth on a long tressle table as she heard her name being called by a group of laughing, excited children.

"Hello, children!" She smiled at the group of former students with genuine pleasure. "Are you excited about the fete?"

That was a question that hardly needed answering, but they nodded enthusiastically.

"Mrs Schrouder!" Jamie, the self-appointed spokesman addressed her. "Mrs Shannon has sent us to you to see if there's anything you need us to do to help."

Dianne loved seeing these eager children waiting ready to do anything to help the success of the day. She quickly sent them to start bringing benches outside to place around under the shade for guests to sit on. She'd hardly finished speaking before they ran off as a pack, laughing and chattering excitedly.

As the morning wore on, it was not just the children who seemed eager to serve. The committee members were there in full strength, deferring to her schedule and list, and several other parents had come along as well, quite ready to do anything that needed doing. Before the scheduled starting time, the school yard began to look quite festive, with stalls set up around about, chairs and benches set in convenient places for sitting to watch activities, and quite a number of bits of coloured paper woven into various patterns, hung from trees, fences and bushes. To add to her already long list of successful beginnings, the day was clear and sunny, and Dianne knew that the townspeople would take the opportunity to come along to the fete and support the school's fundraising effort.

Just as she'd hoped, the yard was soon crowded with school families, as well as many other people not otherwise associated with the school. The stalls were doing a busy trade, the children were wound up like springs, happy and eagerly spending tuppence on some lolly or apple dipped in toffee.

"This is a grand turn out," the Reverend Andrews said to Richard and Dianne as they stood happily watching the day's happenings.

"I'm glad they believe in the school, and their children's education," Richard said, failing to hide his lack of confidence when it came to facing what formerly had been a hostile group of people.

"They believe in you too, Richard," Mr Andrews said, without missing a beat. "It's time you accepted that."

"It feels a little strange, to be honest," Richard replied. "I've been out of circulation for so long, I don't quite know how to act in this sort of gathering."

"Follow the lead of those children," the minister said, smiling.

"Yes!" Dianne laughed. "They don't seem to be held back by any inhibitions, do they?"

"I do feel just a bit presumptuous, though," Richard said seriously. "I mean, I was the one who shut myself away, and who was probably unpleasant, when I come to think of it."

"Well, I preach about forgiveness often enough," Mr Andrews replied, equally serious. "I should hope that all my preaching makes a difference somewhere. I think here is as good a place as any to start."

"I wish I had your confidence," Richard said, just a little weakly.

"It will be all right," Dianne said to him, squeezing his arm affectionately. "Already things are going better than I'd hoped. It will be all right."

And Dianne's prediction was right. The children seemed to be the catalyst needed to break down the misunderstandings that had grown up between the schoolmaster and the community adults. Children dragged their parents to say 'hello' to their teacher, and Richard, no longer burdened by his years of guilt, though tentative at first, soon relaxed into genuine friendly conversation. It all unfolded very naturally.

As the day passed, the stalls once laden with baked goods, preserves and fresh produce were very nearly empty. Hand-made garments and second hand clothing had quickly sold, and the money tins around the ground were full of pennies and sixpences, even the odd shilling.

Children, and even some adults who still thought themselves young, spent more pennies trying to win a small trophy by throwing horseshoes, or bobbing for apples.

It was near the end of the day, when the produce was all but gone, that Peter Todd took centre stage, standing on top of one of the trestle tables. From this position, he began to call the crowd to attention, and issued the challenge for any gentleman, willing to part with tuppence, the opportunity to arm wrestle his way to champion of the day.

All during the day, Peter had taken on the role of organising races for the children: the egg and spoon race, sack races, the three legged race and ordinary flat races. This had occupied them, and caused a lot of good-natured competition. But now, he was calling the adults to compete. Dianne smiled to herself as she saw more than one young man begin to talk to his girlfriend, or wife while rolling up his sleeve.

"This should be interesting," she said to Richard.

"Which strong young gentlemen among you wants to be first?" Peter called, fully aware that he was already provoking egos.

Two gangly lads stepped forward, ignoring the jibes of friends and egged on by the giggling of girls standing nearby.

"Thank you, gentlemen," Peter spoke down to them. "It will cost you tuppence to enter the contest."

The first young fellow threw two pennies down on the table right away, but the other youth looked slightly shame-faced as he realised he didn't have any money left.

"What's the matter young fellow?" Peter asked.

He shrugged, pulling his pocket linings out to show the gathering crowd. "I've already spent everything I brought."

"Here ya go, boy," an older man in the crowd threw the two coins on the table in front of Peter. "Can't miss an opportunity like this just because you don't have the money!"

The crowd laughed, and the second youth grabbed his chance. The two boys turned to listen to Peter as he explained the rules of the game, then they seated themselves, one either side of the table, gripped each other's hand, and tensed their arm muscles.

"On my word," Peter warned. "Go!"

The boys both set at the task of bringing the other's arm flat on the table. Their faces showed the strain of the effort they were putting in, seemingly oblivious to the cheering crowd. Eventually the boy who'd paid his own fee triumphed, bringing his opponent's arm down with a thud on the table.

The crowd cheered, the two shook hands, and the losing contestant walked away. Peter stood next to the winner and held his arm up in the air.

"Now, ladies and gentleman," Peter went about calling the crowd back to attention. "Who will be next to take on our first round winner? Who thinks they have what it takes to bring his arm down?"

Though red-faced, the young man was grinning. He felt the elation of having won, if only once. But Peter knew what he was doing, and he soon had a line of willing contestants, some still in their teens, others older, but no less competitive, and all wanting to prove something for their ego's sake.

The contest continued, the title of current champion changing hands quite a number of times, and the money tin gathering quite a tidy sum. There was a lot of laughing and teasing in the good-natured competition.

"Do I have any other challengers?" Peter called out after some time. "What about some of you more mature gentlemen. Surely you still have strength in your arm to make a fair match of it!"

Dianne was amused at Peter's tactics. She could see he was appealing to pride, and was almost certain that some more men would respond. And she was right. There emerged a new line of older more seasoned champions, showing that years of hard farm work yielded the strength that counted in an arm wrestling competition. And the money tin continued to fill.

"What about the schoolmaster?" someone from the crowd suggested loudly.

"Yes, Mr Schrouder! Why don't you have a go?" Some of the older boys were eager to see what their teacher could do.

Dianne had never even considered that Richard would be a possible candidate, and didn't quite know how she felt about it now that it was a possibility.

"Come on, sir," another student called. "Just for fun. You know we never get the chance to get one up on you!"

"And who says you'll get one up on me this time?" Richard replied in a superior tone, though he was hiding a smile.

"We will never know, sir, if you don't give it a go."

Richard looked at Dianne, almost as if to ask her to think of a decent excuse, but she had nothing to say, so he shrugged his shoulders, and stepped forward. All the students watching were ecstatic, and immediately gave a cheer.

"Well, now," Peter called to the crowd. "Here is a very eligible contestant. I think as he has a large fan club, we should double the entry fee, what do you say, folks?"

Another loud cheer erupted, and Richard was forced to search for another two pence, which he did good naturedly, giving Peter a half-aggrieved look.

He took another look at the last standing champ, and saw he was a fellow of about his own age, but with broader shoulders.

"I don't know that I'm very suitably matched," Richard muttered to Peter as he rolled up his sleeve. "Looks like he tosses hay bales about for a pastime!"

"That is entirely possible," Peter conceded with a grin, "but I'm sure the experience will do you good."

"I'm not so sure that public humiliation is such a good experience," Richard said quietly, as he took a seat, "but there's no backing out now, is there?"

"Hooray for Mr Schrouder!" Some of the more confident students led the others in a cheer.

As Richard took his opponent's arm, and noted the strength he could already feel, he began to wonder how he'd let himself be talked into this.

"I'm afraid there are going to be a lot of disappointed fans when this is over," he said to the young farmer.

"Your fans, Schrouder, not mine!" the farmer answered, already preparing himself for the struggle.

"All right, gentlemen!" Peter called. "At my word. Go!"

Quite suddenly, Richard found himself possessed with a desire to win. He was encouraged by the fact that he had the strength to withstand the pressure exerted by his opponent, and switching his energies to focus on winning, he found that perhaps he was not as outclassed as he'd first thought. The yelling round about reached fever pitch, but if he even heard it at all, it only made him more determined to succeed. He would have been amused to see just how surprised everyone was that he hadn't succumbed right away. Obviously they weren't aware that it was part of his teacher's job description to chop all the wood to keep the school and the school house warm, and also to keep the entire school grounds free of weeds. There was more to his job description than just writing on the blackboard, and that was only now becoming obvious.

Peter was egging the crowd on, and there was a lot of barracking going on, and still the two men remained locked in battle. Even Jillian, who stood close to her step-mother, saw the other children cheering and jumping with excitement, and she herself clapped her hands as if to add her own support to her father's game.

But Dianne began to feel concerned as she watched. She didn't have the same level of competitive spirit that was obvious in both contestants, and she couldn't understand why they would exert so much physical effort, for it caused far too much tension for her liking. *It is only a silly game after all,* she thought to herself. She had just begun to wonder if she would be able to watch any longer when suddenly the match was over. The young farmer had released his hold, and allowed Richard to push his arm flat on the table.

The school children were wild with excitement, jumping up and down, cheering and calling out to their teacher. Jillian clapped her hands, and tugged on Dianne's arm, pointing to her father, wanting her to acknowledge that he'd won. Richard was suddenly aware of the crowd, and what had transpired, and felt quite self-conscious.

"Too good, Schrouder," the losing contestant shook his hand before withdrawing. "Next time!"

Richard smiled in return, but had already decided that it required more effort than he was willing to put in, and drew far too much attention, and he was not only unused to such interest, but a little embarrassed by it. He decided that there wouldn't be a 'next time'.

"Well, that was a good show!" Peter addressed the crowd. "Have we any more challengers, or do we proclaim our school master as the champion?"

There were only a couple of eligible men left, and Dianne heard one of them express their doubt that they would be any good. She was relieved when it appeared that the contest was over. She hadn't liked it much either. It was a bit of fun when it was just the young lads jostling for supremacy, but seeing mature men engage in such an intense struggle was more than she was willing to watch, especially when Richard was one of them.

"Mr Richard Schrouder is this year's arm-wrestling champ, then!" Peter called out, to finalise the matter.

But before the eager students could endorse the call, another voice rose from the crowd.

"Not until he's beaten me!"

The crowd stilled, and parted to allow Edward Jansen to step forward. Richard met Edward's hostile stare.

"Come on then, schoolmaster, let's see who's the better man then, shall we?"

Suddenly, Richard had a flashback memory of the dark night when he'd confronted Kenny's father. That night had left him unconscious and fighting for his life. He'd struggled many times to remember what had actually happened, but now, as he looked into the sneering face of this challenger, recognised that he was slightly drunk as he had been on that fateful night, he knew that Edward had attacked him.

"I'll pass, thanks Peter," Richard addressed the game's referee.

"What's the matter?" Edward taunted. "You yella?"

Richard hid the panic that seemed to be associated with this confrontation, tried to still his racing heart, and ignored the insult.

"I think the contest is closed, Ed." Peter said as firmly as he could.

"It's not closed while there's still a challenger," Edward insisted.

Dianne watched in horror. She also recalled the terrifying night when these two men had clashed, and the devastating result. She felt the blood drain from her face, and she reached for a nearby table to support herself.

"The contest is closed, ladies and gentlemen!" Peter tried to keep his tone jovial and festive, as he had before.

"I want my chance to challenge!" Edward Jansen persisted loudly. "I've as much right to the title as he has!"

"You can have the title, Mr Jansen, by default." Richard spoke evenly. "I forfeit the match to you!"

"No way, Schrouder!" Edward objected. "I want the chance to actually beat you."

"I believe you've had that chance already, on one other occasion, and as I recall, you were the undisputed winner. I'm willing to concede defeat."

Suddenly, Edward withdrew from the centre of attention. He knew exactly what the schoolmaster was referring to, and was sensible enough to know that he'd escaped criminal prosecution on that occasion. He didn't want to focus any attention on that incident.

"What are they talking about?" One woman asked the question that a lot of people were thinking.

"That was certainly a strange response to a challenge."

But no matter how much everyone had an opinion on the subject, the point was the contest was over.

"That was a good money-spinner Peter," Richard spoke to his friend in a low tone, "but a bit too personal for my liking."

"I'm sorry, son," Peter said. "I didn't mean to get you in so deep. What did you mean by what you said to Jansen, anyway?"

"It's not worth going into Peter," Richard brushed the question aside.

Peter was about to pursue it when they were interrupted by a child running up to them.

"Mr Schrouder!" the boy called breathlessly. "Come quickly. Mrs Schrouder has fainted!"

Richard dropped the tin of pennies and raced after the child. Already a crowd had gathered around, and Richard had to push his way through. He saw Jillian first, anxiety all over her face, and she pulled him over to where Dianne lay on the ground.

"What's happened?" he asked Dr Stewart who had attended the incident immediately.

"Not sure at the moment, Richard. Let's get her into the house."

The doctor helped him get Dianne up off the ground, and then Richard carried her past the crowd of concerned townspeople, through the garden gate, and into their own home.

"You see, Muriel!" a man said to his wife as Richard passed by. "I always told you that young teacher was a decent fellow! Never did hold to all that talk you women got up!"

"Shame you don't show me as much attention as he shows her!" the aggravated Muriel replied crossly.

Chapter Twenty-Eight

D ianne woke to find herself safely tucked into her own bed. She relaxed into her pillow, allowing the exhaustion that had overwhelmed her to keep her still and resting. But her mind was awake and active, and she suddenly began to piece together memories of the angry confrontation, which had been the last thing she recalled before fainting. With these memories came a bolt of anxiety, and suddenly her physical exhaustion meant nothing. She struggled to sit up.

"Richard!" she called out anxiously. "Are you there?"

Richard was down the hall waiting in the lounge room, but he was alert. The doctor had made him leave Dianne alone to let her sleep, but he was on tenterhooks, worried about her and the baby. Immediately he came back to the bedroom.

"Lie back, Dianne. It's all right. Doctor Stewart says you are to stay put for at least two days!"

"What happened?" she asked as she fell back on the pillow.

"You fainted, my love. The doctor says you've overdone it...."

"Not to me, Richard! To you - what happened to you?"

"Nothing, sweetheart. I'm all right! See!" He held his arms up for her to inspect his physical well-being.

"But, what about Mr. Jansen? How did you stop him from fighting?"

"Sweetheart! Arm wrestling can hardly be considered fighting..."

"You went against him, then?" Her eyes were round with apprehension.

"No!" He evaded her inquiry, almost in a teasing manner.

"Well, how is it that he backed down?" She was determined to get all the details satisfactorily straightened out in her mind.

"My love!" he brushed her question aside. "Who can think of Edward Jansen when you give me a scare like you did. I was worried clean out of my mind!"

Dianne stared back suddenly understanding that he had been as worried about her as she had been for him, and was a little taken aback by his obvious concern.

"I'm all right, Richard! See!" She lifted her arms mimicking his previous action.

"What about this little darling?" He placed his hand on her unguarded, swollen stomach.

"We're all right - I think!" she tried to reassure him.

"Uh-uh!" he shook his head. "Doctor Stewart has given me strict instructions to keep you here until he's seen you in two days time!"

"But all the cleaning up...." she began to protest.

"Mary-Ann Todd has it all under control. The members of the committee are working like a nest of ants before a storm, following their success!"

"Success?" Dianne asked the one word question, her eyes shining with tears as she anticipated confirmation.

"You did it, sweetheart! We raised enough to get our second teacher!"

Ignoring the doctor's advice, Dianne sat up and flung her arms around Richard's neck, kissing him firmly on the mouth. "I knew they'd help you, Richard," she said breathlessly. "They couldn't fail to like you once they really got to know you!"

Richard couldn't help but smile at her happy, open affection.

"Come on now, Dianne." He thought he'd better calm her down, and obey the doctor's orders. "You're the mother of my baby, and I don't want anything to happen to either of you, so you're going to have to lie down, like the doctor ordered, and don't make me have to get cross with you!"

"You darling!" Dianne laughed at him, kissing him on the forehead again. "I liked you when you were cross, anyway!"

Despite Dianne's victory, she was confined to bed, just as Doctor Stewart had ordered. Once or twice she had tried to get up but each time she found that her body rebelled against the effort. So like it or not, she was forced to do as the doctor said.

Mary-Ann Todd came in regularly to visit, and to help the two men with the household chores. She was full of information about this or that person who'd all but eaten their words about Richard. Dianne couldn't help but smile as she remembered Mary-Ann's attitude from several months earlier, and the dramatic turnabout that had occurred there.

"And you, my dear," Mary-Ann fussed. "How much longer do we have to wait until the baby is due to make an appearance?"

"It's at least another six weeks yet, Mrs. Todd," Dianne told her, sounding frustrated. "I think I will go mad if

Doctor Stewart doesn't let me out of bed soon. And poor Richard! He is trying very hard to maintain the school, but I feel so guilty!"

"Nonsense, child!" Mary-Ann scolded. "Even if the doctor allowed you out, I for one, would not allow you back to work. You have well and truly done your share, and now must wait patiently for your husband to choose a new teacher to help him along!"

Dianne sighed in resignation. "Well, at least I can take comfort in the fact that Mr. Harnen is here to spend time with Jillian!"

"Yes!" Mary-Ann nodded. "They seem quite taken with one another!"

"You don't know what a difference it has made to Richard to have restored the relationship with Helen's kin!"

"I can see the change all right," Mary-Ann agreed.

"He's a different man, Mrs. Todd! All these years he's been hiding behind a facade of bitterness and harshness. The Richard Schrouder I first met is certainly not the man who comes home to me every night. I almost don't know what to do with him! He is so openly affectionate, it takes some getting used to!"

"Don't complain, my dear," Mary-Ann laughed. "You should hear the gossip around town about what a wonderful husband your man is, and I understand there are some other poor men being nagged about not being up to standard. I wouldn't take that too lightly!"

Dianne smiled to herself. She didn't take it lightly. She knew it, and was thankful for it, and oh so thankful to God for bringing her through the dark times and blessing her so much. She had not thought it possible two years ago.

Chapter Twenty-Nine

"Richard!" Dianne reached out and touched her sleeping husband's shoulder, as she rolled over in the dark. She tensed again for a moment as a pain coursed through her. It had been hurting on and off for some time now, eventually waking Dianne from her sleep. But now it had begun to increase in both frequency and intensity.

"Richard!" she whispered again, this time with a little more urgency.

The man lying next to her moaned a little as he was roused from his slumber.

"What....what's the matter?" he murmured, still disorientated, only half awake.

"I think it's time to send for Doctor Stewart!" She delivered the message as calmly as possible, considering the anxiety that had begun to flood her mind.

As Richard understood, he was snapped fully awake. "It's time for the baby?" he asked, a note of panic in his own voice. "Is it coming?"

"I haven't done this before, Richard," Dianne said, perhaps a little shortly, "and to tell you the truth, I'm not sure, but I do know that something is happening, and I'd just as soon Doctor Stewart was here!"

Even while she was talking, Richard got out of bed and

was hurriedly pulling his trousers on, snapping the flexible braces over his shoulders.

"It's moments like this, I regret living way out from the big city," he said. "At least there, they have telephones and hospitals!"

"You won't be gone for long, will you, Richard?" Dianne's tone revealed the uncertainty she felt about the forthcoming delivery.

"I'll send Mrs Todd across, and I'll have Doctor Stewart back in no time!"

"I wish you didn't have to go," she said wistfully, before pausing to bear the pain of another contraction.

"I don't want to leave you, my love," he said hurriedly as he leaned over her to kiss her head, "but there are some things that a husband is not useful for. I'll be praying for you! I feel as if God is actually hearing me these days!"

Dianne smiled weakly as she watched her husband's outline pass from the room. The entire conversation and routine had passed without him taking the time to so much as light the lamp.

"Another cup of tea, Richard?" James Harnen spoke to his son-in-law, who sat staring blankly at the opposite wall.

Richard shook his head. He had been sitting in a similar position for most of the night, and now that the sun had risen and the household had begun to stir, he wondered if perhaps a ridiculous dream had lured him from his bed.

Another muffled cry came from the end room and Richard's body tensed, assuring him that Dianne's agony was no dream.

"How much longer?" he asked again, plainly distressed.

The elderly James Harnen had heard the question, but it was something he didn't know the answer to, and he didn't feel equal to the challenge of being a counsellor, and so he moved on to waken his granddaughter, ready for breakfast.

Just then the end room door opened and Mary-Ann appeared. As she entered the room, Richard looked up hopefully.

"Nothing yet," she said wearily. It was disappointing news and she didn't stop but continued to walk through to the kitchen.

"It's been a long time Mrs. Todd," Richard got up and followed her. "Is everything all right?"

"It's been a while Richard, but I've seen healthy babies at the end of longer labours."

"Do you think it will be much longer?" he asked, heartsick with worry.

"Personally, I don't think it will be too much longer, but I'm not making any promises." She turned from him to retrieve the hot water that had been her original mission, and pushed past him in time to hear another cry.

Richard sat down again, and unconsciously began to twist his fingers. Memories of a similar experience started to flash through his mind, as he recalled the afternoon that Jillian had been born. That day had been long and tense, but there had been the reward and much joyful celebration in the late afternoon. A smile played on his lips as he remembered receiving the tiny girl from the mid-wife. He had been so entranced by the wonder of it all. But with the memory came also a sudden stab of loss. He remembered Helen and the happier times they'd shared before the bitterness had set in. He remembered her, but now he didn't sink into the despair that had caused so much hardness and emptiness.

Instead he thanked God for his daughter, and for the forgiveness that James Harnen had brought with him. Things were going to be very different from now on. Richard knew that for sure now.

He was disturbed from his thoughts by that same baby girl, now quite grown, tapping him on the shoulder.

"MOTHER SICK?" She signed the question.

Richard reached out to his daughter. While Dianne had taught him how to communicate with his daughter, he didn't have the extensive sign vocabulary that she did, and he didn't quite know how to make her understand this new development. He hugged Jillian close. "I wish I knew how to express things to you better," he whispered against her hair.

Jillian pulled back from him. She could feel his lips moving, and wanted to know what he was saying.

"WHY MOTHER STILL IN BED?" She almost demanded an answer with the expression on her face.

"BABY COMING." Richard signed in response, not sure that she would understand. But she understood all right. A light came into her face at the revelation. Dianne had spent a lot of time going through the concept of the new baby, and Jillian was fully aware of what she could expect. She clapped her hands and danced about expressing her excitement.

"She knows more than I give her credit for," Richard said to the grandfather as he entered the room.

"Richard!" Mary-Anne's voice carried down the hallway. "Come on, son, it's here. Come on!"

He didn't have to be called a second time, and scrambled to his feet anxious to be reunited with his wife, and meet his new child.

"Is she all right?" he asked quickly as he brushed passed the stout woman, not bothering to pause for an answer.

"See for yourself, lad," Mary-Ann murmured wearily. "See for yourself."

"Dianne!" Richard looked her over carefully once he was fully inside the bedroom. "How are you ... are you OK?"

Dianne was exhausted and had closed her eyes for a moment or two, but opened them the moment she heard Richard. She smiled at him.

"It's not the best experience I've ever had," she said quietly, causing the frown of worry to remain on Richard's brow, "but it's certainly the most rewarding. It's a girl! See!"

Richard's thoughts were still a bit clouded, worry and lack of sleep getting the better of him, and it took him a few seconds to register the bundle Dianne was tilting in his direction.

"A girl? You had a girl? We had a girl?" he asked, excitement suddenly brushing the fog away.

Dianne nodded slightly.

"A baby girl. Sweetheart, I'm so relieved that it's all over, and that you're all right." He smoothed back a stray strand of hair from her forehead.

"Not half as relieved as I am," she answered with a wry smile.

"What will you call her?"

Dianne fixed her gaze intently on his face.

"I want you to name her, Richard," she said slowly.

"Could I…would it be all right. I mean, you wouldn't mind if I named her…"

"Helen!" Dianne said firmly. "I wish you would name her Helen. For your sake, and for Jillian's."

Tears stood out in Richard's eyes. "For Jillian's sake," he said. "You understand that I am free now. I loved her, and she loved me, and even more, has forgiven me. But I have let her go now. You are everything to me now, Dianne."

"I know," she replied. "I just want Jillian to have a real reminder of the mother she never knew."

"Thank you." Richard couldn't stop the tear that would run down his face, and he didn't bother to wipe it away either, but leaned forward and kissed Dianne.

Then he lifted his new daughter from her, and cradled the infant in his arm, looking at her new features carefully.

"Is she - is she quite normal, Dianne?" The question escaped his mouth before he'd time to prevent it.

"Richard!" Dianne remained calm as she spoke. "Would you love her any less if she wasn't?"

She held her breath a moment while she watched for his reaction. Slowly he bent his head to place a gentle kiss on the baby's head.

"I could not love her any more than I already do, for like her sister, she is already the joy of my heart!"

Dianne breathed a sigh of relief, and relaxed back into her bed. At peace, and with joy in her heart, she closed her eyes and allowed sleep to claim her.

COMING SOON

The Schoolmaster's Daughter

By

MEREDITH RESCE

Despite a hard start in life, Jillian Schrouder has overcome the disadvantage of not being able to hear or speak. Her stepmother has not only taught her how to communicate through the use of sign language, but has also helped her grow into a beautiful young woman.

But despite the fact that she has been introduced into normal society, there are those in the community who simply cannot accept that she is an ordinary young girl who has hopes and dreams, and who has feelings.

Ted Jansen has high respect for his teacher, Richard Schrouder, who is more like a father to him, since his own father is a hopeless drunk. But Ted cannot, or will not, understand that the schoolmaster's daughter is intelligent and quite capable of understanding all the dreadful things he says about her.

Ted has employed the schoolmaster's wife to clean his house while he is at work, and he's happy with the arrangement. But what he doesn't know is that there has been a change, and the person he thinks is his friend and housekeeper, whose little notes of encouragement brighten his day, is actually the person he considers an idiot.